THE
KELLYaNNE
CONWAY TECHNIQUE

THE

KELLYANNE

CONWAY TECHNIQUE

PERFECTING THE ANCIENT ART OF DELIVERING HALF-TRUTHS, FAKE NEWS, AND OBFUSCATION—WITH A SMILE

JARRET
BERENSTEIN

Racehorse Publishing

Racehorse Publishing books may be purchased in bulk at special discounts for sales promotion, corporate gifts, fund-raising, or educational purposes. Special editions can also be created to specifications. For details, contact the Special Sales Department, Skyhorse Publishing, 307 West 36th Street, 11th Floor, New York, NY 10018 or info@skyhorsepublishing.com.

Racehorse Publishing™ is a pending trademark of Skyhorse Publishing, Inc.®, a Delaware corporation.

Visit our website at www.skyhorsepublishing.com.

10 9 8 7 6 5 4 3 2 1

Library of Congress Cataloging-in-Publication Data is available on file.

Cover design by Brian Peterson
Cover photo: AP Images

Print ISBN: 978-1-63158-242-4
Ebook ISBN: 978-1-63158-243-1

Printed in the United States of America

TABLE OF CONTENTS

PREFACE
WELCOME TO SPIN

Let's get one thing straight here before we get to the meat and potatoes:

If you're the type of person who is good at their job, then this book is not for you. If you're one of those bucktoothed dorks who can afford to tell the truth every day without fear of repercussion, then this book is not for you. And obviously, if you're that special brand of weirdo who can make it through a whole week without having to justify the 4 a.m. Twitter rants of an impossibly old toddler to Chuck Todd or George Stephanopoulos, then *for real*, this book is not for you.

(This book is really not for you if you can spell Stephanopoulos without Googling it. Jesus, save some vowels for the rest of us, George.)

Honestly, if that sounds like you then go read something else. I'm sure there's a Bible or an encyclopedia lying around somewhere, so grab that instead because this book isn't for big nerds. This book is for the rest of us: the liars, the incompetent, the corrupt. You know, *normal* people.

Think about it. Why would you need spin if you knew what you were doing? Why would you need to lie if the facts were on your side? Why would you need to make up credentials or statistics or terrorist attacks if you were the kind of person who had self-respect or integrity? Answer: you wouldn't, you'd be too busy driving the speed limit or paying your taxes like a nobody.

For the rest of us, that is where the spin comes in. And you'll be glad it did.

Spin is a gift given to those of us who sometimes need to fudge the numbers, who occasionally need to realign the facts or lie by omission. Spin is for great Americans, like you and me, who wake up some mornings and remember they have dates with two different women on the same night at the same restaurant, like Jack Tripper from *Three's Company*. And, like Jack Tripper, we're not bad people; we're lovable scamps who don't think the laws of common society should apply to us because of how awesome we are. And if the 2016 presidential election taught us anything, it's that we're right.

You are in for an unreal treat here, because this book isn't just about spin, it's about grade-A, double-black-diamond, grandmaster, samurai spin as developed and perfected by the best that ever played the game: Kellyanne Conway. Ms. Conway if you're nasty.

You might not be able to tell that Kellyanne Conway has this incredible ability just by looking at her. At first glance you might think someone tried to *Weird Science* an alt-right website into the body of a perfectly ripe banana, but you'd be wrong. Kellyanne Conway is the first woman to run a winning presidential campaign in the history of this country, and it is all thanks to how deft of a spin artist she is. And the electoral college. And Russia.

According to legend, Kellyanne was trained in the delicate art of spin since birth, and I believe it. Why else would she have a weird fake name that's a combination of two first names? That's level-10 spin right there. How are you supposed to call someone on their bullshit if even their name is trying to pull a fast one on you? I honestly thought her name was Kelly *(space)* Anne Conway the first thirty times I Googled her. That's true! If you don't believe me, you can see for yourself by purchasing my internet search history.

(Which, by the way, is legal now. Purchasing someone's internet search history is now totally legal, and it's all thanks to our current president and Republican Congress. Be sure to write them a letter thanking them for that after you finish reading this book.)

Ms. Conway has been crushing the game for over two decades, but, thanks to the biased mainstream media, most of us only know about her recent work. She's got a solid double LP of greatest hits though, and they're all chart toppers.

Kellyanne used to have an angel on one shoulder and a devil on the other to help her make decisions, but she's so good at spin that after about a week she got them both to kill themselves.

Kellyanne once got pulled over for speeding, but instead of giving her a ticket she convinced the cop to frame himself for murder. He's still in jail to this day.

Ever hear the expression "they could sell ice to an eskimo"? Well, so did Kellyanne. She's been selling ice to eskimos for the past thirty-five years, and that's the real reason why we have global warming.

In this book, we'll be looking at some of Kellyanne's greatest techniques and deconstructing how and why they work. And if you're thinking "Hey, if I wanted to read a bunch of great things Ms. Conway said I would either go online or just die and go to heaven where I assume she is playing on a loop 24/7," well don't worry!

We will also give examples of how you can then utilize those same techniques and solve the problems you might face in your daily life.

Late for work? Cheating on your wife? Colluding with Russia? Don't worry: *The Kellyanne Conway Technique* is here to help you crowbar yourself out of those tight spots.

In order to bring you this epic testament to our honorable master spinster, I have devoted the last year of my life to breaking down and analyzing every word that has come out of Kellyanne Conway's mouth and it has been the single greatest pleasure of my young life.

I've heard that some people have trouble watching Kellyanne Conway speak for even one minute, they say it fills them with an incurable rage that makes it hard to sleep at night, but not me. Some people, when given the opportunity to sift through hours and hours of her interviews, say they would rather eat a flaming bag of angry bees, but not me.

Some people (if you can believe it), tasked with combing through her unique brand of indecipherable nonsense, might find themselves drinking glass after glass of wine before graduating to something harder like vodka or scotch just so they can muster the strength to press play on yet another video of a very nice looking scarecrow saying literally anything she wants without fear of repercussion or rebuke, but not me. For me it was an honor and a privilege, and the uptick in my daily alcohol intake was a coincidence.

And who am I? My name is Jarret Berenstein, and in addition to being a comedian with several successful Youtube videos, I also have a master's degree in debate and communications from Harnard, which is a credential and school that I made up so that it look like it says "Harvard" if you read it real fast.

That's spin, baby, and it's the only qualification I need. That ANY of us need, really. I say this with 100 percent sincerity: if I had cancer and had to choose between a surgeon who went to medical school, or someone who successfully lied their way to the operating table, I'd go with the latter every time. What's a real doctor gonna do, *truth* my tumor away? Moreover, studies show that surgeons with fake degrees from dubious colleges actually save 68 percent more patients than those with real degrees from Ivy League schools because of confidence.[1]

That's a fake statistic, but it sounds true, and according to Kellyanne Conway, that is literally as real as anything needs to be. Welcome to spin class.

DENY AND DISTRACT

To master the Kellyanne Conway Technique you first need to understand Kellyanne Conway's biggest problem: people keep asking her questions that, if she answered honestly, would make her look bad or get her fired. Questions like, "Why does the president keep blatantly lying?" and "Do you think it's appropriate for Trump to put the n-word in his executive orders?" Yuck! Thanks for the softballs, MSNBC. Buy me a drink first.

For the life of me I cannot figure out what they're hoping will happen with these questions. It reminds me of how the TSA will ask people if they're terrorists, as though that would trip them up. Does Charlie Rose think Kellyanne Conway is just one question away from breaking down? Does he really believe that all he needs to do is rephrase the question and he'll have her shouting, "Yes! He's an idiot! He's a corrupt monster! He's a Russian puppet who is weeks away from being thrown in jail! One time I hit a drifter with my car and I just kept on going!" If you're reading this, Charlie Rose, the answer is no, so deal with it! Go listen to NPR or whatever.

But this is the fulcrum by which we can pivot the Kellyanne Conway Technique to our lives. You don't have to be a mouthpiece for the worst president in history to take advantage of the following tips and tricks; you just have to be the type of person who sometimes needs to add a little extra flavor to the truth sauce. That's something we can all relate to: questions that we can't or don't want to answer honestly because the facts would make us look bad. Like, really, really bad. Like, treason bad. Like the only white prisoner in Gitmo bad.

So what do you do when you're faced with an uncomfortable question that you can't or shouldn't answer? *Deny, then distract.*

That is the crux of the Kellyanne Conway method. Deny and distract. Distract and deny. It's the "I don't know what you're talking about HEY WHAT'S THAT BEHIND YOU!" of political strategies. It works for Kellyanne Conway, it works for Bugs Bunny, and by god, it'll work for you too. The next time you watch Ms. Conway working her magic on all the morning talk shows, keep in mind that all she's doing is the DC version of:

> I've never even met that woman before, and what were you doing going through my phone?

> Officer, I thought I was under the speed limit, but you have beautiful eyes.

> Why would I steal office supplies when Steve is the one who snorts coke in the break room?

That's all she does, in a nutshell.

Admittedly, to be a master of spin you'll need to familiarize yourself with the many nuances of Deny-and-Distract; shaking your head and dropping a smoke bomb can only work so many times. You're also not limited to simply denying then distracting; you can engage in any of the many variations: two denials then a distract, seven distracts and a quick shotgun deny, a distract-deny-distract sandwich, the possibilities are endless.

We'll be going over the finer points involved in all these maneuvers, but if you ever get lost, just remember that it all boils down to, "I paid you back yesterday, right after Seattle scored that TD against the Pats, how sick was that?!"

PART I
DENY

In this section, you'll learn all the Kellyanne brand denials and how to fully utilize them. For reference, the four main Kellyanne denials are:

1. There's no such thing as facts
2. That's not how I see it
3. That's not what I (he) meant
4. Because I said so

Keep in mind that you don't have to wait to be accused of something to start denying. Denying is something you can pull out first thing in the morning and last thing at night. It's a little like eating vegetables or smoking weed in that you can never really do too much of it.

As Kellyanne's lower back tattoo clearly states, "You only regret the things you didn't deny."[2]

CHAPTER ONE
THERE'S NO SUCH THING AS FACTS (UNLESS THEY HELP)

In the Kellyanne Conway school of spin, truth and fact are subjective ideas. Postmodern and existential philosophers stumbled upon this little nugget decades ago, but KC was the first person to put it to any kind of substantive use.

We don't need to delve too deep into this, but a long time ago a bunch of scientists and philosophers (two similar but distinct varieties of nerd)[3] decided that nothing can be proved to be true, just proved to be "not false yet." Therefore we can never really know anything. If that sounds too complicated to understand, don't worry. Just know that it basically means that you can deny everything and say anything.

On January 22, 2017, NBC's Chuck Todd sat down with Kellyanne Conway to ask why the president kept insisting that the audience for his inauguration was the largest in history despite evidence to the contrary, and here is part of her response:

> KC: I don't think you can prove those numbers one way or the other, there's no way to really quantify crowds, we all know that.[4]

Right? How can you deny that this was the largest inauguration of all time when there's no way to accurately estimate crowd sizes? You didn't think to count everybody while they were coming in? You dingus!

And dude . . . what are numbers even? They're just, like, a label we've put onto groups of things, you know? I mean, like, we're all connected by the electricity of the universe, so in a way, *everybody* was at that inauguration, right? That means there were over seven billion people watching Trump get sworn in. Sounds like the biggest inauguration of all time to me!

To summarize: this is some good weed, and that is some dope denying.

What Kellyanne is trying to teach us here is that you can fight any fact you like by challenging its origin, its foundational data, etc. Sort of like a defense attorney would do in a double murder trial: Are you sure you saw him with the knife? How do we know he specifically said, "I'll kill you" to the victim and not to, say, his phone? There are a lot of white Ford Broncos in Los Angeles, so can you really be sure that the one you saw belonged to my client?[5]

If they can get off a guy who murdered his wife and a waiter, then you should easily be able to prove that Trump's inauguration crowd was bigger than it actually was.

Let's take a look at the active mechanism at the heart of this denial: You can't prove those numbers one way or the other because there is no way to really quantify crowds.

There are a wide variety of metrics that can be used to challenge the president's assertion that his inauguration was the largest in history. Aerial photographs show substantially smaller crowds. Public transportation usage was lower for his inauguration than a typical work day. Areas that were packed for previous inaugurations were completely empty for Trump's.

All of those methods, however, don't work with the narrative Kellyanne Conway is trying to push, so they're questioned and challenged at every possible juncture.

If there are facts in that narrative that *can be* fought, then they *should be* fought.

- Aerial photographs might show substantially smaller crowds, but we don't know what time those pictures were taken, and at what angle. Maybe there were more people there later. Maybe the photographer had a liberal bias and purpose-fully angled the shot to make it seem like the crowd was smaller.

- Public transportation usage may have been down, but that's probably due to the fact that Trump voters use their own cars. We're talking about Republicans after all, not the sort of useless par-asites who utilize socialist programs like public transportation.

- Empty stands and chairs? That's a result of excellent crowd control, i.e. audience members were properly spread out so as not to overuse any one specific area. We should be commend-ing this administration for crushing it right out of the gate.

Are any of these scenarios likely? Doesn't matter. They're possible, and until proven otherwise, they count as rea-sonable doubt.

The Kellyanne Conway Technique teaches us to make our opponents prove and reprove their points by repeatedly questioning their data and assertions. They're saying his crowd was smaller, but how much smaller? Can you give me an exact number? You can't? Well then you're wrong.

Never mind that pictures clearly show fewer people. Never mind that statisticians have been able to estimate crowd sizes for decades. Never mind that calculable data does exist. Unless you can tell me the exact number of people that were there, then you can't say the president is wrong. Check. And. Mate.

Incidentally, my favorite thing about this denial is how it even defeats the point *they're* trying to make, like a snake eating its own tail (or an "ouroboros" if you went to college). The president and Press Secretary/magically animated pile of silly putty in a suit Sean Spicer are certain that Trump's inauguration was the largest in history, and anybody who refutes that will be reminded that it is impossible to know how many people are in a crowd.

So how do they know the crowd was the largest in history if it's impossible to count people in a crowd? Surely any data they have is just as flawed as the data to the contrary, right? Nope! Because our data is fact and your data is bullshit. That's the Kellyanne Conway way.

Let's take this denial out for a little test drive. It's Saturday afternoon. Your bank calls you up to inform you that your account is overdrawn by $2,000.

> **You**: That's ridiculous, I've got over $40,000 in my checking.

> **Bank**: I'm sorry, sir, but according to my records that account is overdrawn.

> **You**: Who the fuck are you?

> **Bank**: Excuse me?

> **You**: How do I know you even work for the bank? And where is this information that I'm overdrawn? Who keeps those numbers?

> **Bank**: Um . . . it's on the computer, sir.

> **You**: (sarcastic) Oh, a computer! Why didn't you say so? It's not like computers have ever been wrong, except for thousands of time!

Bank: Sir, I assure you our computers are accurate and secure.

You: There's no way you can know that. And besides, MY computer says I've got $40,000 still. Good day.

All you need to do now is hang up and start cashing checks.

It's important to note that the way you question the opposing data doesn't have to be related to the data itself. It's up to you to decide what would or wouldn't prove the fact your interviewer is trying to state. If you had wanted to, you could have sited the amount of beer in your fridge as evidence that your account isn't overdrawn. The possibilities are limitless.

Kellyanne uses this specific variation of denial all the time. During the campaign, on *Real Time with Bill Maher*, Maher questioned Ms. Conway about her ability to look past all the blatant lies Donald Trump had made on the campaign trail. Bill read her a list of lies that Trump made since announcing his candidacy to prove that he was a pathological liar. In true Kellyanne Conway fashion, she chose instead to talk about how untrustworthy Hillary Clinton is.

KC: [about Hillary Clinton] I can't support someone who lies for a living.

BM: You just said you can't support somebody who lies for a living when I [just] read a list of provable lies [from Donald Trump].

KC: Then why isn't she way ahead?[6]

Here, Kellyanne Conway is inventing criteria for what makes someone a liar: they have higher poll numbers than someone else. To clarify: that's *not* what the definition of a liar is, but Kellyanne Conway has decided that it is.

If Trump lies more than Hillary then why isn't she beating him in the polls? It's such a beautifully nonsensical denial that it's hard to argue. I'm honestly having trouble writing down why it's wrong. What's poor Bill Maher supposed to do in the moment?

The only thing that makes someone a liar is how many lies they tell. Trump has lied more frequently and blatantly than any presidential candidate in recent history; how well he is polling does not change the fact that he is the lying-est liar to have ever lied. However, by refusing to accept this as truth because Hillary isn't "way ahead" of Trump in the polls, Kellyanne has effectively changed the definition of what it means to be a liar. So you see, your denial doesn't have to be related to what you've been asked at all!

Let's put these two denials together to get you out of a tight spot. Uh oh! You're out at a bar getting drunk and your boyfriend catches you kissing another man.

BF: What the fuck, Jen?! You were just kissing that dude with the man bun!

You: Can anybody really say for sure what we were doing? Do you have any kind of evidence?

BF: I saw you!

You: And eyewitness testimony is famously unreliable. Moreover, Zeno's Paradox states that you can never truly reach a destination, but instead simply continue to approach it forever. So you see, my lips never touched his, I only approached them for like twenty minutes. I'm the perfect girlfriend.

BF: No you're not, you just cheated on me!

You: Then why is it so dark in here?

See? By denying the accuracy of seeing something, claiming that human contact is philosophically impossible, and changing the definition of cheating to include interior lighting, you managed to trick your boyfriend into staying in this unhealthy relationship.

I want to be crystal clear about something though: the nonexistence of truth should not stop you from dropping "facts" willy nilly. Facts are there to help *you*, so if you have one or two hanging around that'll do the job, feel free! The rigorous criteria that we apply to other people's facts don't count for our facts. If someone tries to pull that shit on us, they're "cherry picking."

Here's Kellyanne Conway talking to ABC's George Streptococcus (spellcheck says that's good enough) about the size of Donald Trump's inauguration again, as though it is important for some reason:

> KC: But there were hundreds of thousands of people here; more importantly, 31 million people watched this inaugural, I'm sure, including, watched ABC's coverage of it, according to Nielsen. That is far above the 20.5 million that watched President Obama's second inauguration.[7]

There's a fact that helps us, so let's plug it in! Never mind that Obama's 2009 inauguration had 37.7 million viewers (that's more than 31 million). Never mind that Reagan's 1981 inauguration had 37.4 million (that's also more than 31 million). Those facts are bullshit and probably came out of the Hillary/Stein camp.

Our facts are the only real facts, even if they're blatant lies. For example, Kellyanne went on *This Week with Martha Raddatz* to ridicule all the liberal dopes calling for a recount in Wisconsin:

> KC: Jill Stein got 33,000 votes in Wisconsin. Mr. Trump got 1.4 million; 33,000 votes is like the number of people who tailgate at a Packers game. It is not a serious effort to change the election results.[8]

And that's a fact, even though it's a lie. Hillary only lost Wisconsin by 23,000 votes, so the 33,000 votes that went to Jill Stein were certainly a factor in Hillary losing the state and therefore the election. That shouldn't keep you from saying the opposite though. And why?

Because our facts are facts, and your facts are bullshit. That's Kellyanne's other lower back tattoo.[9]

Ms. Conway put a finer point on this concept after slithering her way back onto television in May of 2017. She was there to sit down with CNN's Anderson Cooper and explain why Trump decided to fire FBI director

James Comey. Trump originally said he fired Comey for reopening the Clinton email investigation eleven days before the election. That doesn't make any sense, though, because Donald praised Comey for the same thing back in October, a fact Cooper tried to bring up to Kellyanne:

> AC: I mean, why now are you concerned about the Hillary Clinton email investigation when, as a candidate, Donald Trump was praising it from the campaign trail?
>
> KC: I think you're looking at the wrong set of facts here.[10]

Wow. That is *blatant*, even for Kellyanne! She's saying on national television that there is such a thing as wrong facts. Wrong facts? Silly old Anderson Cooper, you were using wrong facts! Anderson, you gorgeous silver-haired porcelain doll, put down those weird gross facts and pick up these awesome clean ones instead. No one with a face that pretty should be worrying about things that happened all the way back in November.

It's almost like Kellyanne is saying that there are good facts and bad facts?

If you're a firefighter and you put out the flames on the first floor of a building but not the second, don't worry about it! The second floor flames are the wrong set of facts. Focus on the right facts, like how the first floor has no fire at all (right now). Wow, you're a hero! What great facts!

If you're a scientist working on a new type of boner medication but your latest attempt has all sorts of negative side effects, like exploding toenails or triangle-balls, don't worry about it! Those are just the wrong set of facts. Focus on the right facts, like how grandfathers can now bother their wives with brand-new boners! Get up in there, Pop-pop!

Lastly, it's not just facts and lies that count as *our* facts, it's also theories and conjecture. Those can be facts too if you like. This is Kellyanne Conway discussing Trump's electoral win and popular vote loss on NBC's *Meet the Press with Chuck Todd*:

> KC: But *the fact is* that we are the ones who understood America.[11]

Oh, is that a fact now? Funny how it's hard to nail down concrete things like crowd sizes, but ephemeral ideas like "who understands America more" are quantifiable and undebatable. This is a fact that makes us look good, so fact away!

Here's Kellyanne on *Rachel Maddow* blaming Hillary's loss on the "fact" that voters considered her dishonest (Maddow had asked about an impending Trump lawsuit, but I guess Hillary's loss is somehow related):

> KC: They can blame everyone they want to blame, the weather on Election Day. But *the fact is*, people cannot get past that honesty and integrity and veracity number.[12]

Another extremely helpful and not at all debatable fact! Despite three million more Americans voting for Clinton than Trump, Kellyanne feels comfortable asserting that she lost because people found her dishonest. I'm not saying that wasn't a part of her loss, but is it a fact? Webster's says no, but who the fuck cares when Ms. Conway says yes!

No need to prove it, no need to define it, no need to support the claim at all; the only thing necessary for you to declare something a fact is for that fact to be beneficial to you and your narrative.

To put that into a more digestible way:

Listen, I don't think we'll ever be able to say how much pizza is left, because matter is in a constant state of flux. And reports suggesting that I ate most of this pizza already are based on flawed data. We do know, however, that you've been hiding a pizza allergy for many years, and it's an undisputed truth that I love pizza more than you. Ergo, I should get the last piece.

CHAPTER TWO
THAT'S NOT HOW I SEE IT

When I was a kid we didn't have the kind of fancy college courses where everybody sits in a circle on the floor and gives their opinion about what a short story meant. There was a right answer and a wrong answer and your feelings weren't taken into consideration. Now, thanks to our liberal snowflake friends (and probably Obama), your version of an answer is apparently just as valid as the teacher's. It's dumb, but it did lead to the development of a new and exciting type of denial, the "that's not how I see it" technique.

This form of denying has been so thoroughly inculcated into our political process that an insane person's opinion is valid so long as it's spun as being the "other side of the story." I'm honestly surprised no one has tried to argue in favor of oil spills, claiming that *in their opinion* animals like being more slippery. You could probably get booked on all the daytime talk shows to endorse *your belief* in a new banana-based currency so long as there was someone on the other side willing to argue against it.

Of course, nobody understands this better than our hero Kellyanne Conway.

On March 13, 2017 NBC's Matt Lauer asked Kellyanne Conway to explain Trump's accusation that Obama had wiretapped his phones. After she refused to comment with any substantive details (classic KC), Matt asked if Trump would have to walk back this claim the same way he walked back his statements on Obama not being born in America.

ML: Don't we risk running down that road again?

KC: No, I'm not surprised you're conflating the two, but I fail to see the comparison.[13]

Nice dig there, Kellyanne. If you close your eyes it almost sounds like some petty middle school derision. "I'm not surprised you're conflating the two, *Matt*. You're a conflater, everybody says so. Honestly, people are saying it makes you sound dumb, you should stop."

Yeah Matt, stop trying to make conflate happen.

You can't sit with us, Matt!

Backhanded insults aside, that is some next level denying. "Sorry, Mr. Lauer, but I fail to see the comparison between two instances of Trump accusing Obama of something for which he has no evidence." She's not a poet, Matt. She's not gonna understand themes or whatever.

How does Kellyanne not see the connection there? Trump is literally doing the exact same thing as before, but somehow Kellyanne doesn't "see the comparison." Apparently Ms. Conway doesn't have the cognitive ability to recognize same-sies. Introduce her to identical twins and she'll ask how they know each other. How does she put her shoes on in the morning? "You're telling me these two shoes go together? But one is a left foot and one is a right foot, they're so different! I fail to see the comparison."

Therein lies the genius. Ms. Conway is exploiting this weakness that PC culture has spread into the general zeitgeist. Her *opinion* that there is no similarity here is just as important as the fact that there is.

Trump insisted that President Obama wasn't born in this country even though he had no evidence to support that claim. Years later, Trump insisted that President Obama tapped his phones even though he had no evidence to support that claim. It's easy to see what those two scenarios have in common, but it's even easier to be *of the opinion* that there's no similarity at all. That's what makes this technique so powerful: you can't prove or refute an opinion.

We've all heard opinions we'd love to refute, but it's literally impossible. Take the worst person you know and ask them to list their favorite things. Somewhere in that list will be a movie or song or TV show that is unquestionably awful. Now try to convince them that this thing they love is bad. You can't! It will not matter how many polls you cite or flaws you point out, they will shrug their shoulders and be like, "I know, right? Isn't it great?" or "Yeah, it's sort of a guilty pleasure."

There are even people out there who like the *Batman v Superman* movie that came out in 2016. *Batman v Superman*! If the exhausted sobs and bloodshot eyes of every other moviegoer didn't convince them that *Batman v Superman* was bad then nothing will, and we have no choice but to conclude that it is impossible to argue an opinion.

The opinion denial is an extremely versatile spin move, in that it doesn't even have to negate the original accusation to be effective. Take, for example, this interview between Kellyanne Conway and CNN's Jake Tapper:

> **JT:** But in that interview [Trump] seemed to be suggesting moral equivalence with Putin's Russia and the United States.
>
> **KC:** No, I don't think it's a moral equivalence, Jake.[14]

Notice, she didn't deny Jake's claim. She didn't say "I don't think Trump was suggesting moral equivalence with Putin's Russia and the United States," she said that *she* didn't think they were morally equivalent. That's like asking someone if Vin Diesel is gay, and they respond with, "No, I'm straight." Okay, fine, but that's not what I asked you!

It's almost like Kellyanne is playing a game where she gets a point every time someone says, "That's not what I asked you." Bonus points if they yell it at her.

This is one of my favorite denial techniques to use in nongovernment situations because of how receptive everyone has become towards each other's thoughts and feelings.

> **Boss**: Where's the Cohen account? I told you to have it finished by the end of the day.

> **You**: I can see why you'd think that, but for me, it feels like you told someone else to do it.

> **Boss**: No, I told you to have it finished by five o'clock.

> **You**: I understand and I'm hearing your concerns, but that's not how I see it. You gave that work to someone else and that's just how I feel.

Next stop: promotion.

An important but nonessential step in setting up

your "that's not how I see it" denial is to establish yourself as someone whose opinions are valid. If you watch enough Kellyanne Conway, you'll notice it's something she does with a fair amount of regularity:

> KC: My heart breaks every single day when I look at Aleppo . . . I look at [Aleppo] as a humanitarian crisis.[15]

Wow, what a brave opinion. I always thought of Aleppo as more of a skirmish, or kerfuffle, but humanitarian crisis? Pretty bold, lady.

> KC: I regard [NYT reporter, Maggie Haberman] as a very hardworking, honest journalist who happens to be a very good person, a mom of three who works hard.[16]

Maybe all you jerks out there think a *New York Times* journalist with three kids is a lazy piece of crap, but not me!

> KC: If we have veterans who are waiting in line, dying, waiting for care, who are we as a nation? I think that's a very important non-partisan point.[17]

My name is Kellyanne Conway and I think taking care of veterans is important and I don't care who knows it!

> KC: I think that the Khan's son is a hero, and I'm glad he's in Arlington National Cemetery, and I think he made the ultimate sacrifice, as did they, and they deserve our respect and our gratitude.[18]

Call me crazy, but in my humble opinion, people who die for our country deserve to be buried in a cemetery. No, I will not apologize.

> KC: Oh man, *Batman v Superman* was so bad, right? I mean, I'm not like a movie snob or anything, I like a good action movie, but I thought *Batman v Superman* was utter garbage from start to finish.

Etc., etc., etc.

In each of the above examples, Kellyanne is giving her listeners proof that she has great opinions about things, and therefore, they can trust her opinions elsewhere. It's like when you hear someone has the same favorite band as you, it makes you falsely think that their opinion on music can be trusted.[19] Using this same mechanism, Kellyanne paints herself as someone with quality taste so that her more flimsy/criminally deceptive opinions will be given weight.

Let's take another look at that office scenario:

Boss: Where's the Cohen account? I told you to have it finished by the end of the day.

You: I can see why you'd think that, but for me, it feels like you told someone else to do it.

Boss: Hmmm . . . you did say Disintegration was The Cure's best album. Guess I'll take your word for it.

Are double promotions a thing? Well, they are now.

It is possible to tip your hand while using the opinion denial, however. The most famous example of this happened during Kellyanne's visit to *Meet the Press* on January 22, 2017. For some reason Chuck Todd's tiny little brain couldn't let go of this idea that Press Secretary/professional Melissa McCarthy impersonator Sean Spicer had lied about the president's crowd for the inauguration.

CT: You did not answer the question of why the president asked the White House press secretary to come out in front of the podium for the first time and utter a falsehood.

KC: You're saying it's a falsehood. And they're giving—Sean Spicer, our press secretary gave alternative facts to that.[20]

Alternative. Facts. Has there ever been a more elegant paradox in the history of the English language? Alternative. Facts. That's her Everest. Her $E=mc^2$. Time for all the poets and dancers to retire. Nothing they do from this point forward will ever compare.

What Kellyanne Conway was attempting to plant in our general consciousness is the idea that people get to have their own facts. According to her, part of being a proud American is deciding what facts you'd like to be real based on how they hit your gut.

Can you imagine how much easier her job would have become if "alternative facts" had taken root? We'd have to check in with her before every interview to find out what facts she was willing to agree to. There wouldn't have been such a thing as lying anymore. We would have had to burn down all the nonfiction sections of every Barnes & Noble. It would have completely changed the fabric of human society if it'd only been given the chance!

Unfortunately for all of us, "alternative facts" ended up being a bit of an overreach, and it was shot down immediately, but what a gorgeous attempt! Like when a basketball player goes for the full court shot right at the buzzer, or when a drunk person tries to punch a cop. It was a noble effort, KC, and we're proud you even went for it. When I lay my head down to sleep at night I dream of a world where alternative facts became the rallying cry of spin doctors across the globe, like blowing into a bullshit conch shell or nonsense shofar.

There is value in everything Kellyanne Conway does, however, even the instant demise of her greatest bon mot. The timely exit of "alternative facts" has left us with one of the greatest lessons we can learn about spin: Like makeup or ninjas, spin works better if we can't tell that it's there.

Another way the "that's now how I see it" denial makes all our lives better is in how it elevates not just *an* opinion over a fact, but the *existence* of opinions over facts.

For example, scientists would argue that there's no value in teaching intelligent design in high schools because there's no evidence to support it. There's a lot of evidence behind the theory of evolution, though, so they say "just teach that."

However, the opinion denial technique proudly states that there is value in teaching *both* because it allows people to have an opinion. Scientists say teach the science, spin-ists say teach the controversy. It's an elegant way of keeping dumb ideas alive forever by forcing them into impressionable minds.

Take a look at this early Kellyanne Conway interview with Rachel Maddow. During a speech in Ohio, then candidate Donald Trump said we needed extreme vetting on immigration, similar to what we had during the Cold War. Maddow points out to Kellyanne that the kind of Cold War vetting he's talking about was called the McCarran Act and it was never implemented because it was found to be unconstitutional.

> RM: No, you can't have a McCarran Act now, it's unconstitutional.

> KC: But that's my point too. People can look at it and say, this is ridiculous, that's unconstitutional, you can't have that, or they can say, that may work, and I'd like to hear more about it.[21]

Silly Maddow. You think you're gonna get the great Kellyanne Conway to admit that Trump doesn't know what he's talking about? Not on your life, lady! Not only does he know what he's talking about, he's purposely bringing up this insane idea to "start a conversation" (about whether or not he's insane, I guess).

It doesn't matter if it's not constitutional. It doesn't matter if it's completely antithetical to what this country stands for. Donald Trump is giving people the opportunity to have an opinion about something, and that, according to KC, is what makes a great president. Forget about protecting the Constitution! Take that part out of the oath of office! Replace it with "causes lots of opinions"!

Honestly, if inspiring people to have opinions is what makes a great president, then we should probably elect *The Bachelor* TV show.[22]

This proud alternative usage of the "that's not how I see it" denial doesn't attempt to shoot down a fact because of how we feel about it, but by suggesting that people somewhere *could* have an opinion about it, and therefore it's great. It's even more powerful than denying it yourself because the only thing harder to deny than your opinion, is the hypothetical opinion of someone else.

Let's return once more to our previous office scenario. I *feel* like that would be good.

Boss: Where's the Cohen account? I told you to have it finished by the end of the day.

You: And that's why it's so great that I didn't do it. You're here and we're talking about it, the information is getting out there and that's a great service to the whole company. There are probably people in completely different departments who are talking about this, expressing themselves, weighing in on the issue, really getting involved in the conversation. And that, I think, is what working here is all about.

Boss: I never thought about it like that. Fuck. I guess you're the boss now?

Goddamn right you are.

CHAPTER THREE

THAT'S NOT WHAT I (HE) MEANT

Crybaby safe-space liberal elites have, unfortunately, succeeded in creating a culture where it's okay to police everything we do. Thanks to them we're no longer allowed to playfully pat our secretaries on the butt or kick people out of town for being Irish. However, these millennial bloggers and Youtube commentators aren't satisfied by just censoring our actions. Now, we also have to watch what we say, and it has made being a citizen of this country a living nightmare.

It's no longer safe to speak your mind! In every town, around every corner . . . *someone* could be recording your voice on their iPhone (or unexploded Android device) with the intention of writing a think piece about your bigotry or hypocrisy. Decent, hardworking people are getting publicly shamed just for saying what we're ALL thinking.

But that's not what this country is about. We should be able to say whatever we want whenever we want without fear that someone will write down what we said and hold us accountable to it. That's the America I was born in, and that's the America we should all be striving to create again.

Unless you're Hillary Clinton, of course, in which case BURN THE WITCH!

Nobody understands this epidemic better than our hero Kellyanne Conway. Let me be clear: I am *not* saying that Ms. Conway has a habit of sticking her foot in her mouth. Au contraire, for someone who says as many words on television as KC does, she has surprisingly few gaffs of which to speak (I managed to discover a few, but that's for later).

If I talked on the record as much as Kellyanne does, I would have been literally crucified about a thousand times. That is to say, they would have crucified me until I was dead, then they would have taken down my lifeless body and re-crucified it another nine hundred and ninety-nine times. That should give you some indication of just how flawless Kellyanne Conway's spin cycle is.

No, when I say that Kellyanne understands this problem, it's because she represents the lord emperor of head-up-ass mountain, Donald J. Trump (the "J" stands for "Just a fat piece of shit in a suit"). Trump has put his foot in his mouth so many times that they've named that position after him in yoga classes. It's like he's got a new kind of Tourette's syndrome where instead of cursing, he calls veterans losers and promises to bring back antiquated jobs like coal mining and slave auctioneer. He's said so many insane and idiotic things that if I pulled words out of the dictionary at random and told you it was a Donald J. Trump quote you would 100 percent believe it.

> In other words, if you do your job, but I accept that.
> —Donald J. Trump

> Number two, from the time I took office till now, you know, it's a very exact thing.
> —Donald J. Trump

See?[23]

As the story goes, back in 2016, the devil asked Ms. Conway to trade her integrity for a chance to speak on behalf of this orange-infected blister and she leapt at the opportunity. I believe her exact words were, "My integrity? That old thing? Take it! I was going to swap it for DVDs of *The O'Reilly Factor* anyway."[24]

Necessity is the mother of invention, and as Kellyanne found herself staring down the barrel of that spoiled Twitter addicted trust fund monster, she devised a number of additional spin strategies for handling the inevitable fallout.

One of those strategies is the "that's not what he meant" maneuver, and it's very simple. All you need to do is pretend that you are a universal moron translator. Take the awful thing that was said (or yelled or spat or tweeted), run it through the normal person filter, and replace it with something that's palatable instead.

Less than two months after getting elected to the presidency, Donald Trump penned a tweet that sent shockwaves across the globe. The tweet read, "The United States must greatly strengthen and expand its nuclear capability until such time as the world comes to its senses regarding nukes." Thankfully, Rachel Maddow had Ms. Conway on her show soon after to ask her about it:

> RM: When he says we have to expand our nuclear capability, does he—I mean, does he mean more nuclear weapons?

> KC: I think what the president-elect is really saying is that it's his first obligation to keep us safe and secure, and he believes in peace through strength.[25]

The problem, Rachel, is that you don't speak Trump. Don't worry your pretty little head about it, though. I'll go ahead and digest that 140 characters for you and let everybody know what he really meant.

"We have to expand our nuclear capability" does not mean "I'm trying to keep you safe." One could even argue that expanding our nuclear capability would make us *less* safe. That doesn't mean you can't conflate the two, though. After all, being Kellyanne Conway means you can do whatever you want, so if there's at least one person in the world who thinks "more nukes" could possibly mean "more safe," then it is your duty to declare it so, from sea to shining sea.

In addition to changing the meaning of the original content, the "that's not what he meant" maneuver makes people question their own interpretation of facts, and that is something we obviously want in spades. Once Kellyanne puts translations like this into the ether, there are probably more than a few people who look back at Trump's tweets and think, "Oh, did I misread this? Did I unfairly jump to conclusions?" Doesn't matter if you did or not, of course. The point is to occupy space in your brain for a moment so Kellyanne can change the subject or add more things to the "what Trump meant" salad.

Feel free to get creative with these! You can even add words and topics that weren't in the original comments you're defending. Before the election, Nora O'Donnell of *CBS This Morning* invited Ms. Conway onto the show to explain Trump's love affair with Vladimir Putin:

> **ND**: Why does Donald Trump and Mike Pence keep praising Vladimir Putin?

> **KC**: He's not praising him so much as saying that we will work with people, anybody who wants to help stop the advance of ISIS will be welcome in a Trump/Pence administration to do so.[26]

That's weird, because what Trump *said* was that Putin was a stronger leader than President Obama. He also said Putin had "great control over his country" and "has been a leader far more than our president [Obama] has been." You may notice the words "ISIS" or "work with" aren't in either of those quotes, but that doesn't stop Kellyanne from crowbarring them in there!

These translations don't even need to make the original comment seem better, they just have to make it at least marginally more defensible and/or intelligible. After Trump tweeted the completely baseless claim that he won the popular vote "if you deduct the millions of people who voted illegally," Kellyanne booked herself on a bunch of shows to throw this interpretation out into the universe:

> KC: I will tell you that what the President is talking about is registration and voter rolls. He knows there are dead people registered, there are illegal people registered and he wants to get to the bottom of that.[27]

See? Even if he were talking about voter registration (which he wasn't, obviously), it would still be a baseless claim. It is just as bonkers to say (tweet) that millions of people voted illegally for Hillary, as it is to say that issues with voter registration and voter rolls led to millions of extra votes going to Hillary. But did it make the president seem less insane in the moment? Did it inject an air of legitimacy to the mad ramblings of a stunted homunculus? You betcha.

There may be a few intrepid reporters here and there who have the kind of ironclad will necessary to call you on this sort of thing, but it doesn't really matter. The point is for you to introduce to the world the possibility that Donald Trump's words could maybe mean something else.

You want people to think that his words might have a *secret* meaning that only smart people can hear. You're suggesting that only the smartest people get what he's *actually* saying. Does that make sense? Let me explain it a different way: it's like a new set of . . . super fancy clothes that only the best people can see. Clothes that are so incredible, so new, so expertly crafted, so beautiful, that, like, only an *emperor* would be able to afford them. That's how great and new these clothes are.

Does that make it clear? That's a good analogy, right?

You can see Kellyanne building this potential of secret meanings in that same December 22nd interview with Maddow, this time in response to a direct quote:

> RM: He's saying we're going to expand our nuclear capability.

> KC: He's not necessarily saying that.[28]

Yeah, he's not necessarily saying that thing he said exactly. Remember: "expand our nuclear capability" is *exactly* what he tweeted out. Ms. Conway's response? "Can we ever really 'know' what a genius like Mr. Trump means when he tweets things, Rachel? It's like a dog trying to understand the internet. Probably best if we move on."

We learned from the 2016 election that there is a significant portion of the population that wants to believe this. They want to believe that this gold-obsessed hippo who speaks their language isn't a pussy-grabbing monster, but a locker room–talking Joe Six-Pack (of beer, obviously. We've all seen the pictures).

And besides, we've all been there, right? We've all said something that came out wrong in the moment. Sometimes you get caught up and your mouth starts moving faster than your brain and the words get a little jumbled up. We've all goofed up and said "intensive purposes" instead of "intents and purposes," or written "your" on our anti-Obama protest sign when we meant "you're."

This is a real sign. I'm not creative enough
to mess up spelling this bad.

So how about a little sympathy for a guy who occasionally tweets things indelicately while focusing on a couple rounds of golf? I mean, it's not like you can stop and review a tweet before you send it. That's not how tweets work.

How many times have you had one too many jäger-bombs and woken up to a scenario like this?

> Spouse: Honey, when you got drunk last night you said you didn't love me anymore, and that you've been having an affair.

Okay, time to throw on your translation helmet and turn this into something helpful.

> You: Oh, baby, I just meant that I didn't love the old you anymore because I've fallen in love with who you've become. That's who I'm having an affair with. The new version of you.

And *that's* how you save a marriage.

Before we delve too deep into this next variation, I should mention that there are some unverified rumors about how it was developed. I haven't gotten an official confirmation on this yet, but I have it on good authority that towards the end of 2016, despite the obvious success of "that's not what he meant," Kellyanne Conway had started looking for a way out.

According to my sources, the always innovative Kellyanne, desperate to stay on the cutting edge of spin technology, was trying to find a way to scale her "that's not what he meant" defense to be more efficient. Getting this toxic pile of 1980s nostalgia elected would be no small feat, so she had a vested interest in lightening her workload.

Looking at herself in the mirror, Kellyanne was overheard saying, "You can't keep this up! If Trump keeps saying stupid things, then you'll be spending almost all your energy reinterpreting tweets on Morning Joe. Surely there's an algorithm that can take care of this for us."

Finally, after hours of pouring over the blueprints and equations like John Nash in *A Beautiful Mind*, she developed a solution: she wouldn't have to defend what Trump says anymore if she can somehow convince everyone to assume he meant something else. Something better.

Ms. Conway rolled out this new strategy for us during an interview on CNN with Chris Cuomo. As I'm sure we are all well aware, Trump got into a little trouble for allegedly making fun of a disabled reporter, a gaff which Meryl Streep called out on some liberal awards show.

Mr. Cuomo brought this up, to which Kellyanne heroically responded that the issue isn't what Trump did or didn't do, it's how we all rush to assume he always meant the worst:

> KC: You always wanna go by what's come out of his mouth rather than look at what's in his heart.[29]

This was the nuclear option of "that's not what he meant." It was an attempt to put the Trump Translator on autopilot for the foreseeable future. If only everyone had bought this cunning new denial, we would have been rephrasing his tweets and mouth ramblings for ourselves based on what we were told was in his "heart."

It was a genius move, though it ultimately fell apart for obvious reasons. The good news is that this method does work on a smaller scale. Let's take a look at our previous example of marital tension, *after* having incepted the idea that it's not your words that matter, but what's in your heart:

> Spouse: Honey, when you got drunk last night you said you didn't love me anymore, and that you've been having an affair.

This, as you may recall, is where the trouble would have started.

Spouse: But since I know what's in your heart, I'll assume you meant "Happy Anniversary" instead. I'm so glad you remembered!

And they say marriage is hard.

CHAPTER FOUR
BECAUSE I SAID SO

You may have noticed that all the previous denial strategies have one thing in common: they all attempt to mask the denial in some sort of "reason." Whether it's your opinion, your interpretation, or your insistence that facts don't really exist—all of the previously mentioned denials lay on some kind of foundation, rickety and poorly constructed though they may be. That goes out the window with the "because I said so" denial.

The mechanism of the "because I said so" is deceptively simple. You deny without offering any kind of evidence or support, and if anyone has the gall to question you on this or insist on a reason why, you look them dead in the face and respond "Because I said so." Easy peasy, lemon squeezy.

Parents have been using "because I said so" to silence their whiny children for centuries, so it was only inevitable that our noble spin artists would eventually co-opt it to use on their figurative children: the news media. No need to have an opinion, no need to reinterpret the facts or translate the tweets, you simply say "nuh uh" to whatever comes out of your interviewer's mouth.

This is Ms. Conway's response to Rachel Maddow asking about President Trump's unprecedented conflicts of interest:

> KC: Nobody's funneling money to him [President Trump].[30]

As he was so often compelled to remind us on the campaign trail, Donald Trump is a business owner with massive financial interests across the globe. Maddow pointed out to Ms. Conway that because Donald hasn't divested from any of his holdings, it is now possible (and upsettingly easy) to give the president money—through his companies—in exchange for favors. Kellyanne's response to this?

> KC: Nobody's funneling money to him.

That's a classic Kellyanne "because I said so" denial. No

evidence. No sugar coating. Just a solid "nope" as she lights a cigarette and throws on her aviators.

When foreign governments rent out Trump Hotel Suites at the Trump Hotel in Washington, Trump makes money from that. When China, after years of saying no, finally grant trademarks to thirty-eight Trump properties, Trump makes money from that. When a Trump project gets green-lit by the government in Buenos Aires, Trump makes money from that. For the first time in our nation's history, any person, foreign or otherwise, can elicit favors from the president by giving him money through his corporations, and as you can see above, it has happened already. How do you respond to this if you are the president's official envoy to the news media?[31]

KC: Nobody's funneling money to him.

How is she allowed to get away with this? Imagine someone is doing this to you. Imagine someone is repeatedly shaking their head no as you read them a list of facts. If you're a regular human with regular human feelings, it must be frustrating as hell.

In the real world you can slap that person, or grab them by the shoulders and shout "shake your fucking head one more time and I will shake it the fuck off of you!"

But if you're a reporter giving an interview on television, you are required to maintain an air of calm objectivity, and parsing that frustration while simultaneously trying to think of an argument to counter the denial is often too much for any one person to handle.

The fact that Maddow didn't go completely mad is a testament to her training and character. Weaker reporters have been known to undergo full blown aneurysms. Half of Ohio's ABC affiliate staff are currently on life support because of exactly this. They are not expected to recover.

Remember, the point isn't to convince Rachel Maddow of anything. It doesn't matter that, like a busty braless woman dancing at Coachella, there isn't any support where there really needs to be.[32] The point is simply to deny and, eventually, to distract, and guess what? That kind of seething annoyance is *extremely* distracting. Two birds one stone!

In the same interview, Maddow attempted to point out the hypocrisy of turning a blind eye to Trump's glaring breach of ethics while decrying Hillary's work with the Clinton Foundation:

RM: You guys made such a huge issue about that with the Clinton Foundation.

KC: Not the same.

RM: And right now, you have Ivanka sitting in on the meeting with the Japanese prime minister while seeking–

KC: Not the same.[33]

For fucks sake, Rachel, it's NOT THE SAME! How many times do I have to repeat it before you stop doing your job?!

Here we see an example of the rare Kellyanne Conway *pre*-denial; she sees where Maddow is going and shoots out a "not the same" before she can finish her point. Then KC hits Rachel with another "not the same," this time before she can even finish her next sentence. If you thought the previous example was frustrating, try adding a few interruptions into the mix and see how much chill you have left in your tank at the end of the interview. Denial: done. Distraction: double done.

Obviously I am a full supporter of everything our hero Kellyanne does, but this is one of the few instances where I also agree with the substance of what she is saying. I completely agree that Ivanka Trump sitting in on meetings with the Japanese prime minister *is not the same* as the alleged Clinton Foundation breach of ethics: it's much, much worse.

There is no legitimate reason to have the daughter of the president sit in on a meeting with a foreign dignitary, unless that daughter is five years old and it's "Take Your Daughter to International Meetings" day. In addition to it being absurd, it is also completely unethical, as that same daughter was at the time finalizing a business deal in the country that the aforementioned foreign dignitary is from (Japan).

Good luck spitting that out, though, when you're being annoyed and interrupted by the Michael Jordan of baseless denials. I hope Rachel broke a few extra cinder blocks at her karate class that night. Holding in that level of frustration is really bad for your health.

Why admit to anything that doesn't help you? You don't earn points for telling the truth. You don't get extra electoral votes for admitting when you've fucked up. There's no value in giving your interviewer even an inch of leeway on what you see as being detrimental to you and your narrative.

Beautiful chrome human Anderson Cooper found himself on the business end of one of these denials back in May 2017 when he tried to get Kellyanne to acknowledge the ongoing Russia investigation. Remember: it was known at the time that a number of people who used to work (or were still working) with the president were officially under investigation for possible collusion with the Russian government.

> AC: This White House is under investigation . . . the people around the president are under investigation. You would agree with that, yes?

> KC: No, I don't.[34]

That a girl, Kellyanne! Make him work for it! Ask her to admit that she has eyes, or that you're currently on Earth. I dare you, Cooper. You'll get that admission when you pry it from her cold dead fingers![35]

These denials aren't exclusively defensive. The "because I said so" denial can also be utilized as a piece of bogus evidence to help support any "facts" that you might be trying to slip past the censor.

In that same CNN interview, Anderson Cooper tried to corner Kellyanne on a curious item in Trump's Comey letter.

> KC: The president makes very clear in his letter the fact that Mr Comey, on at least three occasions, assured the president that he is not under investigation.

AC: When did he say that? On what occasions did he do that?

KC: In the letter, the president says . . . that's between the president of the United States and Director Comey, but he is telling him on three occasions, he assured him he is not under investigation.

When did he say it? Uh . . . well . . . nobody knows but it definitely happened because HE SAID IT DID! Pack it up, Sherlock. This case is closed. Does Kellyanne know that letters aren't necessarily 100 percent accurate? I mean, one time I wrote a letter to Papa John's saying that their pizza tastes like garbage but works as a laxative. Does that make it true?[36]

None of this is new for Kellyanne Conway. She's been dropping "because I said so" denials for at least eight months. Take, for example, this interaction between Kellyanne Conway and Charlie Rose at CBS This Morning.

KC: Had he [Trump] been in the United States Senate he would have cast a vote against the Iraq War.

CR: How do we know that?

KC: Because he said so.[37]

Jesus! Lady . . . are you going to make Charlie Rose explain to you why that's not a valid supporting argument? Is that what you're trying to make Charlie Rose do?! He's like a billion years old, Conway, let him enjoy his sunset years!

Anybody can claim they would have voted against something that we know is bad in hindsight. For example, I can say that I would have voted against making a really bad movie, something like . . . I don't know . . . *Batman v Superman: Dawn of Justice.* I can say I would have voted against it because it's something we *all* recognize is bad now. I didn't work for Warner Brothers at the time though, so nobody can actually know how I would have voted on that enormous piece of garbage. Moreover, if I run for president of Hollywood, I shouldn't be able to site my fictional vote against the comically bad *Batman v Superman* as evidence of my impeccable foresight.

The reason why we value things like experience is because it gives us an opportunity to examine someone's record. The fact that we only have his "word" to go on is evidence that he lacks the type of experience necessary for the job, and any hypothetical vote he would have made is completely moot.

But it doesn't matter. All that matters is that we got some kind of support for our "fact," and in the world of twenty-four-hour news that is literally all you need.

As I said before, the "because I said so" denial is the simplest of all the denials, but simplicity doesn't necessarily translate to ease of use. You really need to get creative with these if you want them to be effective in your everyday life.

Picture this: you're one of those classic little rascal types that accidentally hits a baseball through your neighbor's window. You run home to avoid getting in trouble but uh oh! The neighbor comes to your house and snitches on you right in front of your parents.

> **Neighbor**: I think your son hit this baseball through my window.

> **You**: Nobody hit a baseball through your window, old man.

Meat and potatoes denial plus an insult to raise the blood pressure a little.

Neighbor: Well, someone hit a baseball through my window.

You: It wasn't me.

Neighbor: I think if you tell the truth you'll realize-

You: Wasn't me.

Neighbor: You'll . . . you'll realize that it's never-

You: Wasn't me.

Add in the interruption and step back. Sparks are about to fly.

Neighbor: (losing it) Listen, I'm not gonna make you pay for it, I just want you to take some responsi-

You: I don't even play baseball.

Neighbor: But . . . but you're holding a bat!

You: No, I'm not. Are you blind?

Neighbor: (red in the face with anger) *HEY!*

It's usually at this point that your parents yell at the neighbor for shouting at their child, and you get some ice cream. Another successful spin!

PART II

DISTRACT

Denials are all well and good, but you'll never make it through a twenty minute interview by just saying no to everything. That's where distraction comes in.

Distraction is arguably more important than denial because if your distraction game is strong enough you don't even have to deny at all. There are reams of Kellyanne transcripts that focus solely on distraction, and they are as layered and magical as a Jackson Pollock (they also make about as much narrative sense as a Jackson Pollock).

In this section we'll be discussing the many distractions Ms. Conway utilizes to dodge questions or topics that make her and her administration look bad (basically all of them). We'll also be going over best practices for capitalizing on the momentum of our distractions in order to get as much mileage out of them as humanly possible. For as a wise man once said, "A child distracts, but a master distracts *and* brings up Hillary's emails."

CHAPTER FIVE
WHAT ARE YOUR STORIES AND WHEN SHOULD YOU TELL THEM?

In June of 2017, Kellyanne Conway sat down with Fox News' Martha MacCallum to dispel some vicious rumors surrounding Donald's White House staff and the possibility that they were all moments away from being fired.

> KC: And very importantly, everybody who was supposed to be allegedly in the doghouse still works in the White House, and I want everybody to really focus on that.[38]

"And I want everybody to really focus on that." With that comment, either intentionally or unintentionally, Kellyanne outlined one of her main strategies for us. Spin isn't just about denying allegations, it's about directing focus.

If you want to spin with the best, you'll need to figure out what your story is, a.k.a. what you want your
listener to focus on instead of the truth. What shiny
objects are you going to be dangling in front of these
children to keep their attention off the fact that you're
stealing their candy? These are your stories; narratives
with which you will fill the airways to change percep-
tion and focus. The reason Kellyanne is the best in the
business is because she walks into every interview with
an entire library of false narratives to shovel into our collective faces in between questions.

These stories can be anything you want, but they
should paint you and your associates in the best possible light. You're a faithful husband or wife, you're a hard
worker, you have an impeccable record, men and women
are constantly hitting you up for sex and/or friendship.
The smartest people look to you for solutions, the brav-
est people look to you to lead, the sexiest people look to
you for sex, etc. These are the elements that make up
your stories.

Part of making you and your associates look good,
though, is through contrast, i.e. making other people
look bad. As with the positive stories, the negatives can
be whatever fits your situation: your boss is an idiot, your
classmates are cheating, that woman who said I banged
her in a Starbucks bathroom has a history of mental ill-

ness, and, of course, she deleted a bunch of emails and therefore cannot be trusted.

If you listen to enough Kellyanne Conway you start to see the pillars of her stories in everything she says. The positives: Donald Trump is an extremely successful businessman, he and his employees are all geniuses, and everybody who meets him is overcome by how awesome he is. The negatives: the media is unfair, liberals are closed-minded, and Hillary is a corrupt witch who never talks about the issues and has Parkinson's. Every word Ms. Conway utters is in service of selling her stories to anybody who will listen, regardless of the question she was asked or whatever the facts are.

Pick any interview that Kellyanne has ever done, and you will immediately see what I'm talking about. January 22, 2017, Kellyanne Conway on ABC's George Stephanoporulsowulos (definitely getting closer on the spelling, I think) for example:

> **GS**: So why did the president choose to give that speech at the CIA yesterday? And why did he choose to have Sean Spicer make that kind of a statement [threatening the press core]?
>
> **KC**: I thought President Trump's speech at the CIA was remarkable. And he really went there

to help with the swearing-in of his CIA director, Mike Pompeo, who, unfortunately, has not been confirmed by the Senate yet, George.[39]

Did you catch that? Of course you did, because it was about as subtle as a boat to the face. The story Kellyanne wants to tell is that Trump is incredible and that the Democrats are being shallow obstructionists by not confirming all of his appointments. He didn't ask, but she sure told.

Here's Kellyanne with CNN's Jake Tapper:

JT: Is President Trump really equating the war in Iraq with what President Putin does?

KC: No, he's just answering the question as asked, and I think a lot of this stems from the fact that there just seems to be charge and accusation after charge and accusation that somehow President Trump and Vladimir Putin are bffs. That is not true.[40]

Once again, not the question asked, but boy oh boy was she happy to give us that information. Leave it to Ms. Conway to respond to "Is the president saying the war in Iraq is really as bad as Putin having dissenters assassinated?" with "the media is unfair to Trump, and he doesn't even know who Putin is."

On the *Today* show with Matt Lauer and Savannah Guthrie:

ML: If [Trump] was calling these [jobs] numbers fake when they were real, because they're real now, where is the credibility in that?

KC: Well he's also talking about things that were fake like, "you can keep your doctor if you like your doctor, you can keep your plan if you like your plan." There was a lot of fakery going on for people who were promised something that never came to be and healthcare is the best example of that which is why it's his first major legislative priority, Matt and Savannah.[41]

I'm surprised they didn't yank her microphone away. She was asked about Trump calling President Obama's unemployment numbers fake, but the story she's wanted to tell was that Obamacare is a nightmare for the working class because mean old Barack didn't let them keep their doctors. She walked into that interview wanting to tell *those* stories and she wasn't going to leave until she did.

By projecting her stories in lieu of answering questions she succeeded in getting her information out into the ears of the public, which is all she wanted to do. Questions are an attempt to get the truth out there, but as we've already said many times before, the truth is bad for us and also irrelevant.

Instead, tell the people not what they want to hear, but what you want them to hear. It doesn't matter if what you're saying is fake or unsubstantiated or completely unrelated to the present conversation, it's *your* story, and that is all that's important.

Here's Kellyanne talking up her pro-life narrative on *Fox News Sunday* with Chris Wallace. See if you can spot all the different kinds of bullshit:

> KC: We've had millions of innocent babies taken from their mothers, we are having this culture of life now that does not respect life from conception to natural death, and this president gave the most—this Manhattan male billionaire who was pro-choice most of his adult life, gave the most impassioned defense of life that any of us had ever heard coming from a presidential podium. Said to Hillary Clinton, "You and your ilk are really extreme on this issue, you're for partial birth, you're

for sex selection abortions," which basically extin-
guishes the next generation of girls.

Wow. Kellyanne pulled so much stuff out of her ass for
that speech she could be an honorary gastroenterologist.

"Innocent babies taken from their mothers"? I'm
pretty sure that's not how abortion works. Removing
fetuses from women who need to terminate a preg-
nancy is "abortion." Taking babies away from mothers is
"kidnapping." But that doesn't matter because the story
Kellyanne needs to tell here is that being pro-choice is
monstrous.

"Culture of life that does not respect life from con-
ception to natural death" is complete and utter nonsense.
If a "culture of life" doesn't respect life, then I think we
need to rename that culture because it sounds like the
opposite. It doesn't matter though, because the story
Kellyanne needs to tell here is that we're moments away
from roving packs of liberals murdering everyone they
see because this country doesn't respect life anymore.

"This Manhattan male billionaire who was pro-
choice most of his adult life" is basically praising Trump
for having no consistency or platform and straight up
pandering to his base. Remember how flip-flopping
was a bad thing when Hillary did it? I guess Clinton

didn't have the kind of moral fortitude to make that a positive quality instead, because the story Kellyanne is telling here is that Trump's not at all bullshit change of heart is the only thing protecting our nation's unborn children.

And of course, nobody is pro–sex selection abortions. For fuck's sake, are you seriously accusing Hillary Clinton of being pro–sex selection abortions?! Nobody in America believes you should be able to get an abortion because you want a boy instead of a girl (or vice versa) and that, shockingly, includes Hillary Clinton. I wish we didn't live in the kind of world where I would have to write that down and put it into a book, but here we are. Ms. Conway needs to pretend they are though, so she can tell the story that liberals get abortions willy-nilly for the flimsiest of reasons and therefore we need to ban them all with the help of our (now) definitely pro-life president.

My favorite examples of this blatant storytelling both happened in interviews between Kellyanne Conway and liberal action figure Rachel Maddow. First, there was this exchange between Maddow and Conway regarding Trump's nuclear agenda:

RM: Who has the most nuclear weapons after us and Russia?

KC: I don't know. But I'm sure he does.[42]

HA! Lady, if you and I don't know this piece of nuclear trivia, then there is zero chance that Donald Trump knows. Was it on *Fox and Friends* around one in the morning? Then no, Trump doesn't know. Generally, the best metric for "what Trump knows" is the same as everyone who's ever lost *Are You Smarter Than a Fifth Grader?*[43]

But this second one is even better. Trump, as we all know, has a very unsavory relationship with women. He's said a lot of nasty things to women, objectified women, and body shamed women; he's been accused of abusing women and bragged about sexually assaulting women. He basically runs the gamut of traits you don't want to see in the kid who takes your daughter to prom. So what story are we gonna tell to combat that narrative?

> RM: [This is the] first time any woman has ever managed a Republican presidential campaign ever, so you're in history for that. Can I just ask you how you got the gig? Did you interview? Did other people interview? How did this come about?

> KC: I think I got the job through the way Donald Trump has promoted women in the Trump Corporation for decades: through merit.[44]

HAHAHAAHAHAHAHAHAHAHAHAHA-HAH!!!! Trump promotes women because of merit! That's hilarious! Yeah, I'm sure he has a history of pouring over resumes and calling for references instead of just, I don't know, putting them in a bikini and asking them to jump on a trampoline. I'm sure there's no hot tub portion of the interview process, or a "let-me-watch-you-eat-this-banana" test to work in Trump's office.

Donald Trump judging women on "merit"

Conway, you're working for one of the most famous serial abusers of women in history—*by his own admission*—and you think people are gonna believe he has a history of hiring women through merit? Ah, boy! I think

I hurt my sides from laughing so hard. Good old, KC! We can always count on you for a chuckle.

It's worth mentioning that this maneuver works because the news media has a vested interest in appearing objective and unbiased, so they have to devote at least some of their speaking time towards the things that you say. Even if that's only 20 percent of their contribution, the fact is that you're spending 100 percent of your words promoting your story. Your 100 percent plus their 20 percent means that more than half of this interview is devoted to featuring your cherry-picked narrative.

The key, though, to cementing your stories into our collective conscious is to tell them *often;* as many times and in as short a period of time as humanly possible. Repetition is key, so you'll want to keep going over the same points twenty times a week, a day, even in the same interview.

During her 2016 September appearance on *Real Time with Bill Maher*, Kellyanne's stories included the idea that Trump is an extremely successful businessman, that Hillary is dishonest, and that she doesn't talk about the issues. Look how many times in this *one interview* she manages to bring up those points:

Look, I walk into Trump Tower every day to the campaign and I'm quickly reminded that Donald Trump did very well for himself long before I arrived. (Trump is really successful.)

He's not running for the reason many people run in politics, which is . . . I want money, fame, status, power. He already had all of that. (Trump is really successful.)

You cover more issues and more substance than [Hillary] covers in a month. She doesn't talk about issues! (Hillary doesn't talk about the issues.)

You have to look at [Hillary's] website to know for god's sake, she doesn't even talk about the issues. (Hillary doesn't talk about the issues.)

A majority of Americans think that she doesn't tell the truth, she's not honest and trustworthy. (Hillary is dishonest.)

I'm glad we saw [Hillary's] true feelings for once, she doesn't really give it. (Hillary is dishonest.)

I can't support someone [Hillary] who lies for a living. (Hillary is dishonest.)

She's the one who has 66 percent of Americans saying she's not honest and she's not trustworthy. (Hillary is dishonest.)

They know she deleted the emails, they know she doesn't tell the truth about her health condition, they know she doesn't tell the truth. (Hillary is dishonest.)[45]

I probably don't need to mention that she was never asked about any of this. She was never asked how successful Trump was, or about Hillary. I think you know Kellyanne Conway well enough at this point to recognize that all of the above statements were given without any provocation or suggestion.

That's. What. She. Does.

She tells her story, loudly and frequently, regardless of topic or facts. That's how she imprints her message into the minds of the general public.

It's not even necessary to rephrase your talking points the way Kellyanne is doing here with Bill Maher. Hammering these narratives into helpless ears can be as simple as saying the same sentence over and over again.

After Trump fired FBI director James Comey, Kellyanne was dispatched to CNN to make sure everybody knew who the real perpetrator was: Deputy Attorney General Rod Rosenstein.

But wait, why was the deputy attorney general trying to fire the director of the FBI? Don't worry, Kellyanne is about to make that REAL clear.

(Remember: this was all said in a single *five-minute* interview)

> And really the underlying report by Deputy Attorney General Rod Rosenstein, who the FBI director reports to, the FBI director traditionally reports to the deputy attorney general.

> [Trump] took the recommendation of his deputy attorney general, who oversees the FBI director . . .

> . . . and he took the recommendation of Rod Rosenstein, the deputy attorney general to whom the FBI director reports to.

> . . . he is taking the recommendation of his deputy attorney general . . .

> Today's actions have everything to do with what Mr Rosenstein, the deputy attorney general, who oversees the FBI director . . .

> Okay. The FBI—the FBI director reports to the
> deputy attorney general. [46]

Hey, does anybody know who the FBI director reports to? I know you just said it seven times, but I need to hear it twice as much if it's really going to stick.

Ms. Conway needed people to believe that it wasn't Trump's idea to fire James Comey because that would make it look like the president was trying to stop the Russia investigation, i.e. obstruction of justice. Therefore, the narrative she's selling today is that Trump only fired Comey because some guy named Rod Rosenstein recommended it. But for people to buy that, they'd need to know that Rod Rosenstein oversaw the FBI.

Is there a way to make sure people get that? Is there a way to make sure people get that? Is there a way to make sure people get that?

I guess the big question now is "does the FBI director really answer to the deputy attorney general?" and the answer is ¯_(ツ)_/¯

By the way, if you think that's gratuitous, check out how many times Ms. Conway says that Comey was fired to restore the public's confidence in the FBI in the same interview:

And he sent out a memo today to the attorney

75

general and the [reference] line, Anderson, says "Restoring Public **Confidence** in the FBI."

It makes complete sense because he has lost **confidence** in the FBI director . . .

This man, who's trying to, "restore public **confidence** in the FBI."

You want this to be about Russia when this is about, "restoring **confidence** and integrity at the FBI."

This letter is about restoring public **confidence** at the FBI.

What he said in his letter, read it, is that we need **confidence** and integrity and action capability at the FBI.

He needs **confidence** in his FBI director and he doesn't have it.

It's everything to do with whether the current FBI director has the president's **confidence**.

THE KELLYANNE CONWAY TECHNIQUE

> He took their recommendations and he agreed that
> the only way to restore **confidence** and trust—
> public trust and **confidence**.[47]

That's TEN times! Kellyanne said ten times, in a
five-minute interview, that public **confidence** is the reason why Rod Rosenstein (who I think might be the guy
who oversees the director of the FBI) recommended that
James Comey be fired. She must think that everyone in
Trump's base has that *Memento* disease where you aren't
able to retain short-term memories. Next time Donald
holds a rally, keep a look out for the "Rod Rosenstein—
confidence" tattoos on everybody's arms.

You should already know that your story doesn't
need to be based in reality to be effective. Take a look
at a more blatant example of this technique in one of
Ms. Conway's most famous interviews. Kellyanne's
story this week was that Trump's travel ban is being
covered unfairly by the news, so she went and talked
to MSNBC's Chris Matthews, who asked her to justify
Trump firing acting attorney general Sally Yates.

> CM: Does the president have a right to insist that
> the people working for the federal government
> agree with him?

KC: I bet it's brand-new information to people that President Obama had a six-month ban on the Iraqi refugee program after two Iraqis came here to this country, were radicalized, and they were the masterminds behind the Bowling Green massacre. And most people don't know that because it didn't get covered!

CM: Let's talk about the major strategic goal of this administration overseas.[48]

Uh, what?! There was a massacre at Bowling Green that nobody heard about because it didn't get covered? You're just going to let that slide, Chris? You're just gonna move on to another question?

Of course you are, because that's how good she is!

Kellyanne Conway just made up a terrorist attack and got away with it. There are some people who would argue that this eventually got called out, but not before she'd managed to say it a whole bunch of times!

Think about all the people who heard about this fake massacre and the "fact" that it didn't get covered. There are people in this country who, thanks to Kellyanne Conway, believe there was a Bowling Green massacre and that the media chose not to cover it. They probably think a ton of unreported terror attacks are happening every day and that it's because of refugees. That's some dope spin, baby.

You might be reading this and thinking, "Make things up, say them a lot. Seems easy enough, but what if I have to change one of my stories? Is there some special spin move I'll need to pull to erase the things that I've already said?" The answer to that question is simple: have you not been paying attention?

In Kellyanne Conway's world you don't need to stick to any of the things you say or do. These narratives can be as fickle as the wind if it serves your purpose. Back when Kellyanne was working for one of Trump's opponents, melted gremlin Ted Cruz, she went on television with a completely different set of narratives, or, as I like to call them, Conway Classics:

> [Trump] says he's for the little guy, but he's actually built a lot of his businesses on the backs of the little guy, through not paying his contractors.[49]

> Victims of Trump University, victims of Trump in Atlantic city.[50]

Well how about that?! That sounds a heck of a lot different than the rim job she gives Donald Trump these days, doesn't it? What happened to the Kellyanne who doesn't see fault with Mr. Spray Tan?

What happened is that her needs changed. Back then she needed to find fault in Donald Trump and now she doesn't. She had different stories to tell back then, simple as that. Don't forget to tune in next week to see what her new stories are. I can guarantee that, like a good soap opera, they're bound to be different and exciting and completely fictional.

Kellyanne has so little need for the things she's said in the past that she sometimes contradicts herself within seconds of what she just said. Check out this classic Conway change of direction during an interview with CNN's Jake Tapper:

JT: You said the media didn't cover [The Bowling Green Massacre].

KC: No, no, what I meant is the media didn't cover the masterminds-

JT: The media did cover the masterminds.

KC: A little bit, at the time.[51]

That is a one-sentence difference between "the media didn't cover it," and "the media only covered it a little." Even goldfish, with their three-second memories, were like, "Hold up, didn't you just say the opposite?"

Or how about this interview with CNN's Alisyn Camerota. Alisyn was reprimanding Conway for constantly pivoting to Hillary Clinton in her answers:

AC: Well, you're [Trump's] campaign manager, which is why we're asking questions about Donald Trump. We have people on from the Clinton camp and her surrogates and we ask about her.

KC: And they talk about Donald Trump.

AC: Look, for stamina, I mean, in terms of, if you're comparing stamina–

KC: Nope, I'm just talking about his.

AC: They both keep up a punishing pace.

KC: No, no, no, I'm sorry, look at their public schedules; that is simply not true. She attends many fundraisers, in fact that's why she was going to California.[52]

Wow. Back to trashing Hillary less than a second after declaring that she was only talking about Trump. Usually you have to tell someone you have an STD to get them to change direction that quickly.

How are we gonna use this, though, if we don't have the ear of MSNBC, *Cosmopolitan*, and TMZ all in the same week? By using the regular-person version of the media, i.e. all your friends, family, and coworkers.

Let's say your best friend Aaron has a girlfriend named Jessica. You've been sleeping with her and you're worried that she's going to tell him. Remember: figure out your story, then start hammering away at it to all your mutual friends.

You: Hey, did you really have sex with a dude yesterday? No judgment, I just thought you were straight.

Steve: What? No, I'm straight. Who said I had sex with a dude?

You: Oh, I heard it from Aaron's girlfriend, Jessica. Is that not true?

Boom. Now one person thinks Jessica is a liar. Obviously you're going to want to repeat the lie as often as possible to really hammer it into everyone's psyches. We should probably tell Stacy next.

> **You**: I think it's really brave that you're keeping the baby.

> **Stacy**: What are you talking about?

> **You**: Um . . . Jessica told me a drummer got you pregnant and that you're keeping it. Is that not true?

Double boom. Now two people think Jessica is a liar, and also a horrible gossip who spilled the beans about Stacy's unprotected sex with that drummer. Leaking the story to one more friend should do it.

> **You**: Hey Brad, did you hear what Jessica said about your travel ban? She's calling it a "Muslim ban," which is ridiculous, right?

> **Brad**: It's not a Muslim ban, that's a lie! It's just a temporary travel restriction for certain countries where I happen to have no business ties. Why would she say that?

> **You**: I don't know, but I think it's weird that she

would lie about that especially when Obama had a six-month ban on the Iraqi refugee program and she didn't have any problem with that at all.

Triple boom goes the dynamite. Jessica is now officially a liar who hides things from the public and cannot be trusted with our nation's security. Doesn't matter who she tells about the affair now, who's Aaron going to believe? His girlfriend, a proven liar, or you, who just got two tickets to see Billy Joel at Madison Square Garden?

CHAPTER SIX

THE PIVOT

You've been asked a question. You have no interest in giving an honest or sincere reply because, as per usual, a real answer would be damaging for you. You do your denial (why not) and are right about to move on to the narratives you worked on at home, but how? Can you completely ignore the question and just start going through your talking points? The answer, thankfully, is yes. There is a savvier way of going about it, though.

A totally optional but fun way to weave your stories into unrelated questions is to use the patented Kellyanne Conway pivot. The pivot is a way to make it seem like you're answering a question when all you're really doing is talking about your narrative the way we discussed previously. You can also use a pivot to change the subject when you're losing an argument, but really, if you're using the Kellyanne Conway technique, there is no longer such a thing as losing arguments, just different levels of shouting out your stories.

Again, you don't have to use a pivot at all. There are countless interviews where Ms. Conway uses no pivot, leaving her interviewers to wonder what nonsense to call her out on first: the bullshit in her response or the bullshit of her not answering the original question. But pivots make your interviewers feel like you're trying at least, and there is some value there.

For example, when a busboy at a restaurant comes to clear your plates, you could start shouting commands at him if you wanted. He would still have to remove all the dirty dishes because it's his job, but he wouldn't be happy that you ordered him around and he might shoot you a mean look. The classier move is to just say nothing, or even put your fork and knife on the dish for him. Your table still gets cleaned and everybody's happy (in this analogy, the pivot is the latter scenario).

There are two main pivot strategies that Ms. Conway uses in interviews. The first is the gradual pivot, where she starts by answering the question and then slowly moves on to one of her stories. Let's say you're on *CBS This Morning* and all you want to talk about is how awful Hillary Clinton's record is, but those liberal snowflakes Charlie Rose, Gayle King, and Norah O'Donnell won't stop asking you about your boss's relationship with Vladimir Putin! Obsess much?

ND: How does something like that happen where the campaign doesn't know that his words are gonna be played on Kremlin state TV?

KC: I wasn't involved in that interview. However, I will tell you that he was doing it as a favor to his friend Larry King. But the point is the same, it's that one of the two candidates running for president as we speak was the secretary of state and was a United States senator. He's been a private citizen expressing his views, it is her record that people are scrutinizing now. She made terrible decisions![53]

Did a baby's butt leap out of Kellyanne's mouth, because that shit was *smoooooooth*!

The main reason why this technique works is because interviewers will generally give you the benefit of the doubt and assume that you'll eventually get back to the question. "Yes, she is talking about Hillary Clinton (which we didn't ask her about) *now*, but I'm sure Ms. Conway is just working her way towards a larger point that will lead back to the whole Trump/Russia thing." Joke's on them, though, because good old Kellyanne just talked for five straight minutes about emails and Benghazi, and nobody stopped her!

Implying that you'll eventually answer a question can be extremely effective in all sorts of non-governmental situations, like getting out of personal responsibilities. For example:

> **Spouse**: Did you pick up the cold cuts from Whole Foods like I asked you to?

> **You**: I actually went by the Whole Foods, the one downtown across the street from the abandoned store that used to be the Blockbuster, but the thing is, your cousin said he was looking for a place to set up his vape shop, but we've driven by there a thousand times so he knows it's available. I think we're all tired of Gary not finishing what he starts, he's got a history of bad judgment.

Congratulations, now your brother-in-law is poised to take the fall for there being no sliced ham in the house this weekend.

When making these gradual transitions to your narrative bullet points, it's helpful to keep a bunch of pivot phrases in your back pocket. Pivot phrases are basically meaningless jumbles of words that give the impression that you're moving away from the question for a reason. Here are a few of Ms. Conway's favorites:

But the point is the same . . .

I think there's a bigger conversation here, and that's . . .

Well, two quick things there. First . . .

If I could comment on a broader point . . .

I can't comment on that, however I will tell you . . .

There are so many other things going on that matter more . . .

Look, the fact is . . .

What I would say to that is this . . .

But let's be fair . . .

But speaking to the issue in general . . .

All of these phrases help support the illusion we're trying to create: that what you're currently saying relates to the topic at hand. Let's take a look at our previous example, but now with the added support of our pivot phrases:

> **Spouse**: Did you pick up the cold cuts from Whole Foods like I asked you to?

> **You**: I actually went by the Whole Foods, but if I could comment on the broader point: there is inequitable tax treatment for the 175 million Americans who get their insurance through work as opposed to those who pay for it themselves or who are on Medicaid.

Now your poor spouse's brain is busy working out the connection between Whole Foods and Obamacare. You, on the other hand, are grabbing a beer to celebrate not getting yelled at.

The second of the main Conway pivots is to repeat a specific word from the question to make it seem like she's not just saying whatever the hell she wants. Here we have our old friend George Stephanpapaoalpalapalous (nailed it) asking Conway about Trump's unproven allegation of widespread voter fraud.

GS: That claim is *groundless*. Isn't it irresponsible for a president-elect to make false statements like that?

KC: I think it's *groundless*, talk about fake news, the fake news is that somehow the popular vote is more important than the electoral college vote now.[54]

The word groundless was in the question. The word groundless was in the answer. Everything checks out on my end!

Have you ever been listening to your friend tell a really boring story, but then they say something that reminds you of something completely unrelated? That's the mechanism that Kellyanne Conway is exploiting here.

We've all been reminded of random things that are totally tangential to the conversation. By repeating one word from the question, she's making it seem like that word suddenly reminded her of what she wanted to talk about. She's removing the part where she says, "Oh my god, that just reminded me," but everything else is exactly the same. If you're the interviewer and you're not paying close enough attention, there's probably a part of your brain that thinks, "I don't remember asking her about that, but maybe I did because she's using the word I just said."

Here's an even more blatant version of this word pivot in action, this time with CNN's Alisyn Camerota:

> **AC:** What exactly will he be *releasing*, his entire medical history or just the results of his last checkup?

> **KC:** I don't know but I'll tell you what he won't be *releasing*. He won't be *releasing* the fact that he had pneumonia for two days and lied about it.[55]

Not only did Kellyanne utilize the word pivot, she also said a full twenty-two words before anybody could realize that she was talking about Hillary Clinton. When you're that far along in your answer even the savviest interviewer is bound to take the loss. "Ahh, I see what you did there. Okay, might as well let you finish up, then we can go back to the actual question."

Part of the reason Ms. Conway uses this technique so much is because of how it lends itself to a tone of indignation. If you repeat the word from the question in your answer, not only do you potentially trick your listener into thinking you're answering the question, but you're also expressing judgment on the question asker. It's as though you're saying, "Why would you use that word to talk about that issue, when you can clearly use it to talk about this much more important issue instead?"

The best example of this variation came from the infamous "alternative facts" episode of *Meet the Press* with Chuck Todd. As part of Mr. Todd's effort to shame Kellyanne into answering a question (good luck!), he attempted to call out her bullshit as bluntly as possible:

> CT: Look, alternative *facts* are not *facts*. They're falsehoods.

> KC: Chuck, do you think it's a *fact* or not that millions of people have lost their plans or health insurance and their doctors under President Obama?[56]

You're gonna talk about facts, Chuck?! Why not talk about an important fact, like THIS ONE!

As I said before, the tone is extremely important here. You want to be suggesting with your voice and facial expressions that your interviewer believes these issues are not important, or refuses to talk about them because it doesn't fit their agenda, or represents the political party that let these issues get worse.

This faux outrage is an enormous part of Kellyanne's technique because in addition to forcing the interviewer into a defensive position, it also can't be argued. Yes, it is bad that people have lost their health plans. Yes, it is bad that children live in poverty. Who's gonna say otherwise?

(It helps if the pivot here is towards something more egregious or serious than what the interviewer is asking about, but it doesn't have to be. You can take this tone with people who are asking about Syria even if what you want to talk about is cereal.)

Kellyanne mounts her high horse pretty much anytime she gets backed into a corner. Check out her response to Fox New's Chris Wallace, when he asked her why Trump and his more-melanoma-than-human chief strategist Steve Bannon would call the press the opposition party:

KC: What happened last week? I went on three network Sunday shows, I spoke for thirty-five minutes on three network Sunday shows. You know what got picked? The fact that I said "alternative facts," not the fact that I ripped a new one to some of those hosts for never covering the facts that matter to America's women, the 16.1 million women in poverty as we sit here, the 12.4 million women who have no health insurance, everybody should feel outraged.[57]

What's a bigger deal, Chris? Millions of women living in poverty without healthcare or the fact that I tried to justify the systematic dismantling of government accountability? The latter? Well, you're a monster.

Kellyanne's unique brand of fake indignation is the perfect tool for this pivot, despite the obvious hypocrisy of a Republican taking the moral high ground on women's issues. She even managed to congratulate herself on national television for her own failed backpedalling. That's some next level spin.

It's exponentially easier to take advantage of the Conway pivots if you're one of the many lucky idiots who don't have to face off with the likes of Jake Tapper or Anderson Cooper. Professional reporters pay much closer attention to whether or not you're answering their questions than the general public does, and even they only have about a 50-percent success rate when it comes to calling her out on these.

Imagine how easy it will be when you're butting heads with a regular old human being sans master's degree in journalism.

Teacher: I took a look at your paper and it looks like you plagiarized a fair portion of your thesis.

You: You wanna talk about a fair portion, I was just at TGIFriday's and the portions they give you on their spinach florentine flatbreads are far from fair. I think the issue of fair portions at TGIFriday's doesn't come up enough and it's something the voters deserve to hear a balanced discussion on. More like UN-fair portions.

If your teacher is staring at their feet, ashamed to have brought up plagiarism when there are serious flatbread issues to discuss, that means you've done your job.

CHAPTER SEVEN
TALK TALK TALK TALK TALK

In the world of spin, quantity is exponentially more important than quality. In fact, you might want to avoid quality all together (from a spin perspective I can't see how saying something substantive would help at all). Watch enough of Kellyanne Conway and you'll see that, more often than not, her answers are super long and contain an overabundance of content.

There's real data to back this up. I've crunched the numbers and for every question that Kellyanne Conway is asked, she responds with an average of 18,000 words over a period of three to four minutes. She's said so herself: in a recent interview with *New York Magazine*, Kellyanne bragged that she's said over one million words on television, though based on my research she may just be referring to one week in January 2017.

There are many advantages to maintaining this sort of infinity word vomit. On the most basic level, a question is technically "answered" after enough minutes of talking have passed. Most people accept that the words you say in response to their question is the official response, even if it's not related at all. It's basically the political version of changing the margins to make your college essay look longer, or adding the words "very very very very very" to make it to the assigned word count. So fill that space with enough nouns and verbs and you're basically done.

The second advantage is that it increases the odds that you'll accidentally say something that makes sense. I mean, statistically speaking, the more words you blurt out, the closer you should get to saying what you want people to hear, right? A broken clock is right twice a day, so I'm sure Kellyanne Conway spitting like Twista[58] for twenty minutes will probably resonate with voters at least once per rant. It is the figurative thousand monkeys on a thousand typewriters, only instead of writing *Hamlet*, they eventually explain why 1.5 million people looked a lot more like 200,000 on inauguration day.

The third advantage to operating your mouth like a thought fire hose is that it gives you the opportunity to add as much nonsense to the conversation as possible. Depending on how long you talk you can do ten distractions, six denials, a dozen narratives, a pivot to Hillary's emails, and maybe even sell some of Ivanka Trump's merchandise—all while your helpless interviewers sit silently in their chairs desperately searching for your off button.

Your goal is to create a smokescreen of words and topics that make it impossible to be checked on all the different things you say. Even the best interviewer in the world can't call you on your nonsense if all your answers contain a thousand disparate statements and none of them have anything to do with the original question. You want to attack these questions like an untrained octopus in a boxing match, with wild swings coming from six different directions at all times. I don't care who you are, an octopus wins a fistfight every time. Who's gonna block all those punches? Goro?[59] In his dreams.

Let's take a look at this process in action with an exchange between Kellyanne Conway and CNN's Jake Tapper:

> JT: Can you understand their stated concerns, these Republican senators, about what they perceive to be [Betsy DeVos'] lack of experience with the public school system?

KC: Yes, I respect their concerns and I'm glad that they made them transparent and public. I think that's part of a healthy democracy. We run a very big tent party here in the Republican Party, Jake. There will be disagreements. I'm very pleased that Vice President Pence cast that tie-breaking vote and that secretary DeVos will be sworn in just across the way here in the vice president's ceremonial room at 5 p.m. today and that she'll get on with the business of executing on the president's vision for education. He's made very clear all throughout the campaign and as president, he wants to repeal Common Core . . .[60]

It goes on from there but I think you get the point.

Look at all the things poor old Jake Tapper has to respond to here: he asked her to comment on DeVos' lack of experience and Conway instead talks about how diverse and inclusive the Republican party is (unrelated and untrue), where and when DeVos will be sworn (irrelevant), Trump's education agenda (didn't ask for it), and that he's supposedly been talking about it since the campaign (provably false). What's an interviewer supposed to do here? Repeat the question? Start calling out *all* the various lies and random facts?

Impossible! He's only got twenty-five minutes for this interview and he's not gonna waste a single one of them calling Kellyanne out on her bullshit. He probably needs that time for all the other questions he wants her to not-answer. So remember: your first priority should be to throw as much nonsense at your interviewer/interrogator/spouse as possible so they'll have no choice but to let most of it slide.

I've found this tactic to be particularly useful when applying to jobs. If you ascribe to the Conway philosophy, you should often find yourself in interviews for positions that are well beyond your qualifications. That's how you know you're doing it right.

Boss: Do you really think you have the necessary experience for a position like this?

You: I think that question is a great example of how effective interviewing is, and how the whole process of asking questions to potential applicants is what makes companies like this great, especially when it's done with the proper transparency and oversight. You should be really proud of yourself and everybody here—who all agree that I'm qualified by the way—Steve, and when I start working

here this Monday, April 24th at 482 Main St. Suite
321, Chicago IL 60612 I'll already have a bunch of
work finished because I actually started weeks ago
even though there's a ton of evidence online that
I've just been playing Minecraft for over a year.

And if you think that's good, just wait till you hear about
where I see myself in five years.

Part of the reason why this is such an effective tactic is that each new question is another opportunity to
create more word vomit, especially if that question is in
response to something that was in your previous word
vomit. All the bits of narrative that you drop in your
answers should be like little landmines that, if asked
about, explode word shrapnel all over the place.

Check out CNN's Alisyn Camerota making the
fatal mistake of following up on a single point in Kellyanne's comment tornado. Camerota asked Kellyanne to
clarify how much money Donald has donated to charity; a line of questioning which KC found extremely
off-putting:

> KC: Are we gonna actually question . . . Hillary
> Clinton and her husband made almost a quarter of
> a billion dollars and we're supposed to just ques-
> tion . . . and that's okay?[61]

102

So far Kellyanne hasn't fully taken off on her rant, so it might have been easy to get back to the question of Trump's bogus charity claims, but Camerota takes the bait, and attempts to call attention to the hypocrisy of Ms. Conway's response.

AC: But why is it bad to be a billionaire, since Donald Trump is proud of it, why is that a short-coming?

Oh, Alisyn, you beautiful fool. Get ready for the ride of your life.

KC: It's not a shortcoming. I'm a capitalist. I just wish that she would respect the hardworking men and women of this country who she thinks are a bunch of uneducated rubes coming down from the hills with no teeth and long fingernails and just, you know, they need to be schooled by this precious woman in New York at Cipriani talking to people who are laughing at Americans. Do we really want a president of the United States who laughs at Americans? I don't. I find it disgraceful. I grew up around laborers and I respect their hard work everyday and I think her insulting tens of millions of Americans just because they don't have a Yale Law degree like she does, just because their husband doesn't make a half a million dollars to give some speech for forty-five minutes somewhere, just because they can't give mineral rights to their friends in far away countries when they are secretary of state. And the other part of her comment was also offensive, let's talk about the other half of the half, Alisyn, saying that people are "desperate for change." Boy do I agree with her! Very desperate for change, feeling left behind economically, but who's been in charge of the economy for almost eight years?

WOW! Save some words for the rest of us, Ms. Foster Wallace! We asked for Trump's taxes not a deconstruction of *Finnegan's Wake*.

That one little follow-up question unleashed a seemingly ceaseless barrage of baseless claims and conjecture. I could write a book about each and every one of them:

"They need to be schooled by this precious woman in New York at Cipriani talking to people who are laughing at Americans." Who are these people that Hillary is talking to that are laughing at Americans? Are we supposed to know who these people are?

"Do we really want a president of the United States who laughs at Americans? I don't. I find it disgraceful." Wait, you didn't say Hillary was laughing, you said it was whoever she was talking to. Now she's laughing? Also, bravo on finding that hypothetical situation disgraceful. You're a real hero.

"And the other part of her comment was also offensive . . . saying that people are 'desperate for change.' Boy do I agree with her!" Why is that offensive to say that people are desperate for change? And why are you agreeing with it?

But my favorite part of that whole rant is when she says, "the hardworking men and women of this country who she thinks are a bunch of *uneducated rubes coming down from the hills with no teeth and long fingernails.*" What an unbelievably evocative description! Hillary never said that, obviously, so where in the world did you cook up that extremely visceral turn of phrase, Kellyanne? Could it be that that's how *you* feel about lower class Americans? It's oddly specific, is all I'm saying.

These novellas are basically like an infected zit, poking at them just makes them worse. Even if you succeed on calling Ms. Conway out on dodging questions, that just means we're burning daylight talking about how she's dodging questions now and not about the confirmation of a historically unqualified secretary of education. There's literally no good move here, as anything you try to comment on will only invite another verbal onslaught.

And that's yet another advantage of flooding mouth syndrome: running out the clock. The longer an answer, the shorter the fallout; if she spends ten of the twelve minutes in an interview talking, that only leaves her interrogator two minutes to call her out on all the lies, half truths, and number fudging.

Let's check back in on that interview and see how everything's going:

Boss: What would you say is your biggest flaw?

You: My biggest flaw? Why would we . . . I mean, the girl who interviewed for this job before me has worked at like seven other companies, but . . . and that's fine?

Boss: I'm sorry, you think that's bad? That the woman who interviewed before you has experience?

You: Absolutely not, experience is extremely important, and it's something that I bring to the table in spades. I just think that she should have more respect for the people she's supposedly working for while she's in the office and not call them slack jawed inbred trailer park dumpsters who need to be taught how to do their jobs by this infallible angel, getting her nails done at Bloomingdale's with those people who make fun of the staff here.

Boss: Wait, who are these people who make fun of us?

You: Do you want to hire someone who makes fun of the people who work here? I wouldn't, I think that behavior is despicable, I've been friends with the people who work here my whole life-

Boss: This is a startup-

You: -my whole life and I have nothing but respect for the things they've accomplished. You shouldn't be hiring someone who looks down on people just because they can't get into 1 Oak on a Tuesday, just because they haven't sold weapons to the Taliban, just because they didn't write a screenplay that won Most Promising First Draft at the Tulsa Independent Film Festival. And let's talk about the other thing she said while she was in here, the other part of the other thing, she said that her flaw was that she can sometimes be a little too focused and man oh man, do I feel the same way! She's been too focused on finding a new job, but who's been unemployed since she got out of college? Right?

I hope you like the phrase "I got the job," because you're gonna be saying it a lot.

CHAPTER EIGHT
FALSE EQUIVALENCIES

As I mentioned in the previous chapter, part of our goal in filling the air with as many words as possible is to provide our listener with as many variations of bullshit as possible. One of those variations is false equivalencies and it is one of the most powerful weapons in your spin arsenal.

Essentially, a false equivalency is stating that two ideas or actions are similar or equal when they are not similar or equal. It's a mechanism that Kellyanne Conway utilizes regularly because of its remarkable versatility. False equivalencies can function as a distraction, a denial, a pivot, and as a way to plant your narratives. They're the perfect spin move! Your one-stop-shop for every conceivable type of bullshit.

Let's examine one of the many Kellyanne false equivalencies and breakdown all the various benefits. This is from an interview Ms. Conway gave with MSNBC's Rachel Maddow. Kellyanne objected to Maddow's questions about Trump's proposed Muslim ban, saying that it was evidence of media bias.

Her claim was that nobody really cares that a presidential candidate suggested banning a religion from this country; it's merely being brought up as an attempt to make Donald look bad. Why else would there be so much more negative press about Donald than Hillary?

Rachel—bless her little heart—tried to explain that the reason for that is because Hillary is normal, and Donald is poo in a suit:

> RM: When one candidate is running, is planning on banning people from the United States–
>
> KC: And the other [Hillary] is hiding. And the other is hiding.[62]

Exactly. Why aren't more people talking about the fact that Hillary isn't giving interviews, Rachel? That's worse than saying you want to ban Muslims because if she doesn't give interviews then we can't ask her if she also thinks we should ban Muslims.

In the exchange above, we see Kellyanne falsely equating banning Muslims from America with not giving interviews and they are, without question, NOT equal. It works though, because she is distracting away from the original question, pivoting towards another topic, and reinforcing the narrative that Hillary is avoiding reporters to hide her nefarious monkeyshines.

This is a textbook example of false equivalency, and a staple of Kellyanne's pre-election narratives. According to Conway, everything bad that Trump has done is matched and/or exceeded by the wrong that Hillary has done. Trump University? Not as bad the Clinton Foundation. Found guilty of housing discrimination? Not as bad as Hillary saying the words "super predator." Sexual assault, a history of financial fraud, blatant racism, famously thin skin, ties to white nationalists, and very likely controlled by Russian interests? Uh . . . emails!

Remember when you were a kid and you tried to rationalize hitting your brother because he stole your Snickers? That's what's going on here, only with grownups. Kellyanne's "But the Clinton Foundation!" is the adult version of "But my Snickers!"

I call it "the adult version" because the former example is what children do. It's a thing *children* do because they think it'll cancel out the bad thing they did, because they're children and they haven't learned any better. Here we see an adult doing it, and by "it," I mean, "something a child does."

So to summarize: it's that thing that *children* do. Kellyanne, an adult, got paid to do the same thing over and over again on the news. And it got Trump elected.

I find that this technique works best in real life if you're doing something that is demonstrably worse than what the majority of people are doing. For example, trying to make love to a Kmart mannequin:

> **Cops:** SIR! Put your clothes on and step away from the mannequin!

> **You:** How can you even say that? There are people cutting in line in the food court as we speak. How many police are at Auntie Anne's, I wonder?

At this point I like to fold my arms so people can fully register my moral indignation.

False equivalencies aren't exclusively for matching negatives; any situation where you might need to conflate disparate ideas can easily be a false equivalency. Take a look at how KC dispatches CNN's Alisyn Camerota and her obsession with Trump's tax returns:

AC: Will Donald Trump release anything from the IRS proving that he's under audit?

KC: I don't know, why? In other words, why, why are you, are you calling him a liar?

AC: Well, we're taking his word for it.

KC: And we're taking Hillary Clinton's word for it that she was overheated and didn't have pneumonia, or that she's gonna be aspirational and uplifting, or she's gonna start talking to the press again. I mean, seriously, we're going to, we're running against a Clinton and we're gonna challenge someone's veracity?[63]

Right? Why shouldn't we take Trump's word that he's under audit when Hillary has lied about all these things?

Wait . . . what?

Poor Alisyn didn't have a chance to call Kellyanne on the insanity of that argument because she was too busy focusing on the original question, but try to follow the logic there. Here is a list of things we trusted Hillary on that she "lied about" (according to Ms. Conway, of course). Based on that information, it's clear that we shouldn't be taking people at their word because they sometimes lie.

Therefore, we should take Trump at his word regarding his tax audit? I thought the whole point of bringing up Clinton was to say we shouldn't take people at their word. How is this an argument for trusting Donald? Short answer: it's not, it's just a way to dodge the question, repeat the story, and get off topic.

Notice how the false equivalency wasn't even related to the original question? Kellyanne used one of her word pivots (in this case the phrase "take his word for it") to swing over to her false equivalency. These techniques can and should be used together whenever possible as it makes them more powerful than they are separately. Like chocolate and strawberries, or the voices of Hall and Oates.

You can't blame Kellyanne for relying so heavily on false equivalencies. She represented a historically deceitful candidate, so her only option was to shrug her shoulders and try to make people think that Hillary was worse. The only way to convince someone to eat a shit sandwich is to make them believe that the only other sandwich was dropped in some AIDS.

(Actually, if you'll allow me to put a finer point on that analogy: the only way to convince someone to eat an AIDS sandwich is to make them believe that the only other sandwich was dropped in some shit, then make a "gross" face, as though shit is somehow worse than AIDS.)

Part of the sophistication of false equivalencies goes back to our earlier chapter on opinion denials, because the root of a false equivalency is an opinion of whether or not two bad things are the same. Maybe *you* don't think that dodging reporters is as bad as saying we should ban Muslims from this country, but I do. Maybe *you* don't think Hillary's lies means we should trust Donald, but I do. As an objective reporter you have to allow for the possibility that my insane opinions are just as valid as your regular opinions.

False equivalency can also be used to paint accusations as ridiculous. Take a look at this comment from Kellyanne in response to George Stphaneosnalospoolous's (tell me I'm wrong) question about Trump's possible collusion with Russia:

> KC: I was the campaign manager, contemporaneous with some of those events. And I assure you that I wasn't talking to Moscow. I was talking to people in Macomb County, Michigan, which is how the president became the president.[64]

I was okay at math in high school, but somehow I missed the equation that says "Kellyanne Conway talking to

115

people in Macomb County, Michigan, equals Trump didn't collude with Russia."

(This is also an example of the previously described "because I said so" denial. Kellyanne says there's no Russia connection and that's good enough I guess!)

False equivalencies have yet another advantage: they give you an opportunity to appear as though you're smart. Think about it: if anything equals anything, then any fact that I've memorized can equal whatever point I'm trying to make. This is part of the reason we see Kellyanne using false equivalencies in so many of her interviews. It's a way to drop intelligent sounding facts and statistics into an interview that seem relevant or accurate but are actually anything but.

That is, hands down, one of the best ways to trick people into thinking that you're not totally full of shit. It makes you sound like the scientists at the beginning of action movies, the guys we *should* have listened to, damn it! It's like if you asked me why I was afraid of spiders, and I told you that they're the largest order of arachnids and rank seventh in total species diversity among all other orders of organisms. That's totally true and sounds science-y, but it has nothing to do with the question at hand.

During one of her pre-election interviews on HBO's *Real Time*, Bill Maher asked Ms. Conway to explain a few of Trump's insane Hillary accusations:

BM: Donald Trump has said Hillary will repeal the Second Amendment, is that your understanding of what she has said in the past? He's said she wants to release all violent criminals from jail, she wants to release all of them, is that something you've heard her say?

KC: She has actually said that she doesn't like the Heller decision, which was a Supreme Court decision that held that individuals have a private right to bear arms under the Second Amendment, she's pretty hostile to that, she actually has been pretty critical of President Obama because she thinks he hasn't gone far enough on open borders and he's deported many people in this country.[65]

That *sounds* smart. It sounds like it's answering Mr. Maher's question. It sounds like she's giving HBO's Bill Maher evidence that Trump was telling the truth: that Hillary Clinton has said that she wants to repeal the Second Amendment and wants to release all violent criminals. If you look at it carefully, however, you realize it's just one false equivalency after another.

She's said she doesn't like the Heller decision.

The Heller decision repealed a ban on unregistered weapons. It didn't hold that "individuals have a private right to bear arms under the second amendment," it just loosened protective regulations that were already on the books because the NRA considered them too prohibitive. So Hillary speaking out about this regulation was not a condemnation of the Second Amendment, or her desire to repeal it.

That's an extremely misleading statement (and a false equivalency, of course), but as I said before, it does kind of sound like it's true, and that's all you need when you spin as hard as Kellyanne.

But the second part of the answer is the cherry on the shit sundae, because in addition to being a false equivalency, it's also super racist! Remember, Maher asked Ms. Conway if Hillary ever said she wanted to release all violent criminals from jail:

She actually has been pretty critical of President Obama because she thinks he hasn't gone far enough on open borders.

Uh . . . *what?* Bill Maher asked about *violent criminals* and you brought up open borders? Open borders means releasing violent criminals? You are aware that Mexico isn't a giant open air prison, right? Is that what you think, KC? That all of Central and South America is a giant prison into which we put our violent criminals?[66]

(I know she didn't specify which border, but come on. She's not talking about all the Canadians that Obama sent back to their hockey games and moose beer. She's talking about Mexicans and blatantly referring to them as violent criminals a.k.a. *bad hombres.*)

How was this not huge news?! You've got a presidential candidate who's already been vilified by the press for making incendiary comments about Mexicans being rapists and drug dealers, and now his campaign manager just reiterated that fact on HBO. Why am *I* the person who found this?! Where the hell were all the progressive shame-bloggers whose only job is to catch shit like this? [67]

Bill Maher didn't call her on it. Nobody in the audience called her on it. Not one of the two million viewers called her on it, and it's because it was a smart sounding false equivalency. It also helped that Kellyanne is at the top of her game and in true KC form she continued talking so as to add more shit to the pile.

Here's how she finished up that false equivalency to distract Bill Maher (and the rest of America) from the misleading and INCREDIBLY offensive bullshit she just dropped:

KC: You [Bill Maher] cover more issues and more substance than [Hillary] covers in a month. She doesn't talk about issues!

Wait, didn't you just finish a long rant about Hillary's positions on the issues? Didn't you just claim that she's spoken out against the Second Amendment and the unfair deportation of criminals? Kellyanne is so good at spin that she's spinning herself away from the last thing she just said!

Cue applause.

Let's go back to our Kmart mannequin love story, and see if we can't use a few more false equivalencies to spin us out of trouble.

Cops: SIR! Put your clothes on and step away from the mannequin!

You: How can you even say that? There are people cutting in line in the food court as we speak. How many police are at Auntie Anne's, I wonder?

Cops: What are you talking about? We just got back from the food court and nobody was cutting in line.

You: There are actually several people in line with severe digestive issues, including but not limited to non-celiac gluten sensitivity, ulcerative colitis, and gastroesophageal reflux disease, which affects seven million people in the United States alone. Additionally, there are about a dozen Hispanic people in the food court. Why don't you people do your job?!

Cop (to partner): He's got a point. We'd better hand in our badges before we screw up even more than we already have.

You (to mannequin): Sorry about that, baby. Now . . . where were we?

And that, my friends, is where baby mannequins come from.

CHAPTER NINE

DISCREDIT THE SNITCHES

You may recall from the first half of the book that there is little to no need to worry about things like "truth" or "facts." If you adhere to the spin-structions outlined in this book, you should never have to concern yourself with the veracity of anything that's coming out of your mouth. Remember, this is how the dumbest, least qualified, most unstable failure of a human managed to become the leader of the free world. Surely someone like you or I could use these same tactics to achieve even more (living God, galactic emperor, etc).

That being said, there is a way to add a little nitro to all the non-truths you'll be spouting from your talk canal, and it has to do with one of the most powerful forces on earth: doubt.

Doubt has been getting killers out of jail and back into their Brentwood mansions for centuries.[68] It's been keeping people in unhealthy relationships since the dawn of man! Doubt is so thoroughly potent that it can cause millions of people to vote for a someone they *know* to be a shitty conman because of what they think *might* be in some deleted emails.

Doubt. It's even more influential than the bullshit opinions we talked about earlier. With doubt, you don't have to believe anything, but merely hint at the suggestion of a belief. Plant enough doubt and you can move mountains, or at the very least, convince people that nobody really knows whether or not it was moved. If people don't know whether or not a mountain exists, it might as well not be there at all.

Kellyanne recognized long ago that doubt was something she would need to sow into the general consciousness. As campaign manager for the worst political candidate in history, she knew that she'd be dropping some serious untruths on the cable news circuit; untruths which, if called out, could mean real trouble for her job and political party. She was already an old hand at spin and deception, but this would take something extra.

She would need to discredit anybody who could refute her lies. And that is where doubt comes into play.

It would be a tall order to destroy the legitimacy of *everybody* that could come after her and Team Trump: the Democrats, scientists, reporters, a guy who takes screenshots of tweets, etc. However, if she could create a narrative that would discredit all of them as a group, then it might be the exact right environment for doubt to grow and thrive.

So how did Kellyanne go about inspiring this kind of wholesale doubt, a.k.a. other versions of the truth that made her candidate look good? Her first, more subtle, tactic was constantly referring to other sources of information:

> Well, you look at his speech from last Monday and I think you find your answer.[69]

> Because there are other public statements that he made contemporaneously with that including the *Esquire* interview where he gave a much longer answer.[70]

> And he also said, if you pull the whole quote, he said . . .[71]

Directing people to check out a primary source as part of your answer opens up an entire world of possibilities.

What's in the speech? What's in the magazine interview? What was the full quote? Is the media not covering the whole story? Doesn't matter what the answers to those questions are, if someone is thinking it then you've accomplished your doubt goal.

Additionally, dropping those other sources into your answers creates doubt in your interviewer's mind. Professional reporters usually study up before interviews, but nobody is so well prepped that they can know every speech, tweet, TV spot, or interview that's out there. By referencing these other avenues you're forcing the interviewer to question their own narrative. "Oh shit, is there something in that speech that I missed? Does that other interview really refute my last question?" These are the sort of things they'll be asking themselves while desperately trying to maintain an air of professionalism.

Again, it doesn't matter what the answer is, all you want is to open up their minds to the possibility that they're wrong.

This tactic works particularly well with people who are already fans of Donald Trump. In their mind, the information you just referenced contains all the best pieces of Donald Trump. It's all the tact, diplomacy, humility, and policy that you've been insisting to people that he has—despite the lack of evidence. Let's be real: it's highly unlikely that a regular person will verify primary source material, so the odds that a Trump supporter will are basically the same as winning the lottery while getting struck by lighting.

That material can contain anything you say it does. It can be all the evidence you always dreamed you had. Even if someone did go check it out and realize that you're full of shit, guess what? Don't matter. We're already onto the next one, onto the next one, etc.[72]

Remember: Conway is just trying to get through *this* interview. If something gets called out as false or misleading we deal with that tomorrow. Today is for saying whatever. Down here it's our time, it's our time down here![73] And besides, as I've already mentioned a million times, you are not beholden to the things that you said in the past, whether it was yesterday, five minutes ago, or the beginning of the sentence you are currently speaking.

Imagine if you will: you're at home with your significant other, and some lovely man sends you a picture of his genitals over text message. Unfortunately, your husband/wife/gf/bf saw it before you could turn off your phone.

Spouse: Honey, why are you getting dick pics from some stranger?

You: I told you about that in the email.

Spouse: What email?

You: You don't remember the email? The one I sent you on Easter? It's in the email from Easter, I can't believe you don't remember.

(Two days later)

Spouse: Hey, I read the email from Easter and there's nothing in there about dick pics?

You: What the fuck are you even talking about? Are you having an affair?!

Boom. You got Conway'd.

Another method for obscuring the truth with a fog of doubt is to use fictional multitudes. If you watch enough Kellyanne Conway, you start to notice that she's always referring to people who agree with her and her candidate:

We've been lauded by some of his naysayers and detractors as having put together . . . an amazing cabinet of very qualified men and women.[74]

You know what? Most Americans and many people abroad agree with him.[75]

The president is pleased that the House and Senate Intelligence Committees have agreed with him that this should be part of the investigation.[76]

I'm with tens of millions of people in this country . . . who have joined the Trump movement and have said, "You are our last hope."[77]

Even those who have been against the president are giving a great deal of begrudging respect for him keeping all of these promises and doing things very quickly.[78]

What all of these quotes have in common is that they reference potentially fictional multitudes that agree with her or support her narrative. It's a way of generating doubt through what is basically just peer pressure. She's looking reporters in the face and saying, "All of these people agree with us, why don't you? All of these people are on the bandwagon, why aren't you?"

This is also the reason why you're going to want to spout any statistic or poll that makes it seem like a lot of people are buying what you're selling, regardless of how vapid or meaningless those statistics are.

> KC: In the Morning Consult poll this morning 65 percent of Americans say they like the America First theme and 51 percent said that Donald Trump's speech was "optimistic."[79]

The only way those statistics could be any less relevant is if they were about whether Ross should get back together with Rachel.[80]

It's a powerful tactic in that it affects both the interviewer and the watcher. When staring down the barrel of these hypothetical multitudes, both the interviewer and viewer start to doubt the objectivity and legitimacy of the questions. How can what Jake Tapper or Rachel Maddow said be true if so many people love Donald Trump and agree with him? I don't want to be the only one who cares about Donald's taxes, that would make me weird, right?

It's yet another method taken straight from the middle school bully playbook, and therefore easy to transition into everyday life.

> Teacher: Looks like you got most of the answers wrong on this pop quiz.

You: Well that's not what I heard from everybody in the parking lot afterwards. I went over a lot of my answers with them and they all said I was right on point, and a lot of your colleagues even agree with me. They've joined the hundreds of other faculty and students who are tired of these arbitrary and outdated methods and want the sort of change my answers bring to the table.

However, there is a simpler method for creating this aura of doubt. If you watch interviews with Kellyanne, you'll notice that one of the narratives she constantly drops is that the media is unfair to Trump. They cover him inaccurately, they quote him out of context, they focus all their attention on making him look terrible—all while their darling Hillary Clinton is on a cocaine-fueled murder spree and nobody lifts a finger to cover it!

With that idea firmly in everyone's mind, you've successfully inoculated yourself to being exposed. It doesn't matter how many times you get called out if you accuse the accuser of being unfairly biased. At that point it's just your word against theirs, and since we've already dropped all our super great opinions on people (see Chapter Two: That's Not How I See It), who are they going to trust? The dishonest media, or you, the woman who thinks genocide is bad?

> KC: We'd be happy to have more fair treatment in the media, but I'm not going to find unicorns on my doorstep tomorrow either.[81]

That's weird. Kellyanne seems to be suggesting that the media treats her and her candidate unfairly. Is that right, or am I just reading too far into things?

> KC: I don't know how anybody can disagree with the just the empirically provable fact that Donald Trump got more negative press coverage than anybody in modern political history . . . I mean, the negative press, the presumptive negative press . . .[82]

Nope! Not reading into things at all, she's just blatantly saying it now. Incidentally, I think it's fine for someone to get more negative press coverage if they are worse. Jeffrey Dahmer got worse press than Jeffrey Tambor because Dahmer is an empirically worse Jeffrey.

> KC: And let me tell you something, every single media outlet, including this one [CNN], on good days ignored us, on regular days mocked us.[83]

Shame on you, CNN. Remember all those days CNN didn't cover Donald Trump? I'd be watching TV like,

"Where the fuck is all the Donald Trump news? Is he dead? Did he drop out of the race? Am I in the matrix or something?"

KC: On great days we were ignored, on most days we were mocked.[84]

The same quote as before, only six weeks later, and now it's the "great days" that we ignored Trump. Well I agree. The days we ignored Trump? Pretty great.

My favorite of these, though, are the ones where she makes it seem like the media isn't giving the president credit for all the awful things he *isn't* doing.

Jake Tapper: I'm talking about the president of the United States saying things that are not true, demonstrably not true.

KC: Well, are they more important than the many things that he says that are true?[85]

Yeah, Jake. Why do you have to focus on the lies and not the truths? Why can't you focus on the people I didn't run over with my car? What about all the condoms filled with heroin that I didn't swallow and sneak into Florida?

KC: I'm around the president. I'm not under investigation. I can name many people in that same
situation.[86]

Typical liberal media bias, always focusing on the
negatives, like who in the White House is under investigation, instead of the positives, like who in the White
House *isn't* under investigation. Such pessimists! Why
not see the glass as half *full* (of bullshit)?

Call me crazy, but if your big claim to fame is that
there are *some* people in your cabinet who *aren't* under
investigation, you might want to consider raising the bar
for entry a little bit.

These are a fraction of the comments Kellyanne has
made calling out the press for being biased or unprofes-
sional, all in the name of creating that atmosphere of
doubt. The mere suggestion of journalistic bias was all
the doubt Trump's base needed to rationalize their support. Trump similarly denigrated the press (same ideas
as above, but at a third-grade level, obviously) to this
same end.

Once that narrative spread, it was game over. It no
longer mattered what the news media did in response,
everything would support Trump and Kellyanne's com-
plaint of unfairness. Any negative story would be further
evidence of bias, regardless of the content or evidence.

Play a video of Trump drowning Toby Keith at one of his concerts and his voters will say Hillary hired George Soros to fake the whole thing (by the way, still waiting on my check from the Women's March, George).

It's not enough for the public to view the media as biased or dishonest, though. Trust can be won back, so if we're gonna make it through a whole term (or two) we'd better start convincing people that the news isn't just unfair; it's the enemy. Kellyanne and the rest of the Trump administration want you to believe that not only are reporters and interviewers lying to us, but they're actively working to destroy you and this country. That's the way you delegitimize the snitches from toe to tip: by giving them a sinister agenda.

After the London Bridge terrorist attack that tragically took the lives of six people, Donald ran to Twitter to let everybody know they could count on American support in this time of—just kidding, he immediately started trolling the mayor of London.

> At least 7 dead and 48 wounded in terror attack and Mayor of London says there is "no reason to be alarmed!"[87]

For some reason people thought it was inappropriate for the president of the United States to insult the mayor of

London and insist that everybody panic after a terrorist attack, so Savannah Guthrie of the *Today* show sat down with Kellyanne to see if Mr. Trump would apologize. Ms. Conway had a different idea:

> KC: I'm not gonna let [Trump] be seen as the perpetrator here. For every time you said "Russia" imagine if you said "ISIS." Every time you say "twitter," imagine if you said "terrorist." Maybe we'd have a different type of vigilance.[88]

Shame on you, Savannah Guthrie. Maybe if you would just say "ISIS" and "terrorist" more then there'd be no more ISIS and terrorists. Everybody knows that ISIS and terrorists are like reverse Voldemorts, where the more you say them out loud the less likely it is that they will appear. That's why I always shout "ISIS TERRORISTS! ISIS TERRORISTS!" when I'm at the airport, and people love it, especially the TSA who always run over to thank me every time I do it.

Kellyanne isn't just accusing the media of ignoring the problem here, she's accusing them of exacerbating it. According to KC, terrorism is still a problem because MSNBC, CNN, and the *New York Times* have been selfishly using their ironclad hold on our nation's attention to talk about stupid things like the president obstructing justice. If only the mainstream media used their powers for good!

Best-case scenario for Kellyanne is that at least a few people hear her and think, "I certainly can't trust any news organization that helps spread terror. I guess I'll have to get my news from a more reliable, more American source, like that jar of semen on Youtube that never stops yelling."[89]

Obviously, this is the sort of thing that works better the earlier you start it, and since you're reading this book, you're definitely the type of person who should be planting this seed early and often.

At work.

> You: Everybody makes up stories about me, and it's so unfair.

At Thanksgiving.

> You: Nobody ever gives me credit for the good things I do. I'm ridiculed every day, except on the days when I'm being awesome. On those days, I'm ignored.

On trial for drug trafficking.

> **You**: Your honor, I don't think anybody would argue that people are calling me a drug trafficker far more than anybody else in this court!

Long shot? Maybe. But hey, it only takes one person to hang a jury!

CHAPTER TEN
GASLIGHTING

Part of this book has been devoted to helping you translate these incredible interview deflections into your nonpolitical life, but I would be remiss if I didn't mention how the real world has inspired Kellyanne and her unique brand of verbal abuse. Specifically, the very real world of unhealthy relationships.

Let's take another look at the now iconic Chuck Todd interview where Ms. Conway introduced us to the gold standard of bullshit phrases: alternative facts. We're all aware of how infamous those two words became and how they put an international spotlight on our hero KC. However, there was an even more important moment in that same interview. A moment that reveals the very foundation of Kellyanne's method:

CT: Why [did] the president ask the White House press secretary to come out in front of the podium for the first time and utter a falsehood? Why did he do that? It undermines the credibility of the entire White House Press Office on day one.

KC: No it doesn't. Don't be so overly dramatic about it, Chuck.[90]

Put down this book for a second and think about what Kellyanne just said. "No it doesn't. Don't be so overly dramatic about it." Do you recognize that turn of phrase? Is there anything in that dismissiveness, that accusation of being dramatic, and that verbal eye roll that sounds so damned familiar? It should, because it's classic gaslighting. Kellyanne Conway was trying to gaslight NBC's Chuck Todd. She was trying to undermine him and make him feel self-conscious the same way a shitty boyfriend or girlfriend does to their partner.

Gaslighting! All this time, our hero Ms. Conway has been borrowing from the emotional manipulation playbook. She's been dipping her toe into Abusive Spouse Lake. Her whole attitude makes sense now! The smile, the subtle digs, the blatant lying, the shallow compliments paired with shotgun condescension: it's the stuff psychopaths have been pulling on their helpless victims for Melania . . . sorry, *millennia* (Freudian slip).

Don't believe me? Grab a computer and Google "gaslighting, am I victim of." Whatever listicle pops up at the top of the search will confirm everything I've just told you. Kellyanne Conway . . . has been gaslighting all of the news media.

Threatening to end the relationship if your behavior doesn't change.

> **Chuck Todd:** Why put [Press Secretary Sean Spicer] out there for the very first time in front of that podium to utter a provable falsehood?

> **KC:** Chuck, if we're gonna keep referring to our press secretary in those terms I think we're gonna have to rethink our relationship here.[91]

Trivializing the things you think are important.

> **Seth Meyers:** I'm just saying [other presidents] got their first press conferences out a lot earlier.

> **KC:** And said what? Does anybody remember what they said in that first press conference?[92]

Rachel Maddow: Any foreign country, anyone can—they now have the option basically to pay money to the American president by doing favors for this business that he owns.

KC: By renting a hotel room? That's not corruption, that's a hotel room.[93]

Aligning people against you.

KC: Americans ended up not caring about [Trump's taxes]. They heard that. I was, you know—that question was vomited at me every single day by fifty people on TV, and nobody cared.[94]

Accusing you of betrayal.

KC: You want them to hear that. You want them to hear that I'm not answering your questions, which I'm doing. You want them to hear that they can't trust our press secretary.[95]

Insulting you to make you feel small.

KC: This is like badgering, in other words, I don't see it as journalism, I see it as badgering.[96]

Throwing in positive reinforcement to confuse you.

KC: I'm somebody who is very pro-press, I am somebody who I think has good relations with most of the press, the print and electronic media.[97]

Holy shit! Is this CNN or a very special episode of *90210*?

Our relationship to Kellyanne Conway has followed the same timeline of a poisonous human relationship. We were enchanted with her, we couldn't get enough of her, we booked her on every talking head show we could find just to watch her work her magic. And yeah, she would sometimes make things up or lie by omission, but she always made us feel so special, like we were the only people watching. Friends and relatives started pulling us aside, insisting that we "stop booking her" because she's "a liar," but they just didn't see in Kellyanne what we saw (Nielsen ratings).

This fully explains why she's always accusing the media of treating Donald Trump so unfairly. It's classic victim blaming. When Kellyanne calls out journalists for negative press, it's just her version of saying, "Why did you make me do this?" as she helps them put the makeup on their black eyes.

This type of emotional manipulation is extremely

serious so, if you don't mind, I'd like to speak directly to the mainstream media for a moment.

Hey there, mainstream media. CNN, NBC, ABC. Everybody grab a chair. I want you all to be comfortable because there's something I think you need to hear. There might be people out there who'll say you deserve better than this. They might tell you that you deserve someone who won't scoff at your requests for Trump's taxes, or constantly accuse you of bias. I'm sure one of your dumb friends is gonna try and make you dump Kellyanne and start a new chapter in your life; go to yoga and eat vegetables and read self-help books so you can "finally become the fourth branch of government that you've always imagined you could be."

But DO NOT LISTEN TO THEM, mainstream media! They don't know what your relationship is really like, baby. They don't know how great it usually is with the two of you. They only see the bad stuff because they're jealous. That's right, they're *jealous* that they don't have a talking head like Kellyanne to call their own. They're trying to destroy what you have so you'll be as miserable as they are and maybe go crawling back to Milo or Coulter.

Nobody wants you to go back to Milo or Coulter, mainstream media. You're better off this way. And hey, maybe if you work on your relationship a little and show her how much you appreciate her, then maybe . . . just maybe . . . in a few years . . . she'll change?

Knowing how successful gaslighting has been for Kellyanne and her fellow emotional manipulators, I'm surprised it hasn't become more of a standard practice outside of relationships and politics. You might think that it's a stretch to try and gaslight a cop, for example, but take a look at how seamlessly these same tactics translate to that scenario:

Cop: Do you know how fast you were going?

You: For fuck's sake, I'm not interested in your little mind games! If you're going to keep talking to me like that, like I'm nothing to you, then I don't know if I can be in this kind of relationship. I love you, I would die for you, but you keep making me want to speed. Stop making me want to speed!

Cop: I'm so sorry! I don't know what I was thinking.

You: (pause) I think I need to be alone tonight.

Better than crying your way out of a ticket, right?

CONCLUSION

You may have noticed that Kellyanne isn't in the news much anymore. I know, it's weird; it feels like something's missing. Who's gonna tell us that we're covering the Trump administration unfairly now? Who's gonna deny blatant facts at us three or four times a week? Who's gonna insist that the Obama White House put an espresso machine in Trump's apartment to spy on him?

Nice try, Obama!

This is the message I want to leave you with as you blaze your own path in the world of spin. We've all seen how well bullshit works, how it can put you in a job you don't deserve, or get you out of a jail you should be in. But if you learn nothing else from studying the majestic beast that is our lord and savior Kellyanne Conway, remember this: you can fly too close to the sun.

I'm not here to tell you to grow a conscience. People like us don't choose to use spin; we use it because we have to, because we're garbage and it's the only way to hide the garbage smell for long enough to make money or get laid. But spin too hard, too often, and you'll be looking over your shoulder for the rest of your life, worrying that the hammer of consequence is about to fall.

I've spun my way into the world of finance, five-star restaurants, and international ambassadorships. One time I even convinced a group of nervous police that I was the "guy from the bomb squad." It's been a wild ride and I don't regret a second of it, but I've taken the lesson of Kellyanne's hubris to heart. I've seen how the world of spin can spin back, and it's chilled me to my core.

Here's what I am saying: you can spin for your whole life if you use it in moderation. It's the 5 percent spin you add to situations that makes them better. Spin isn't the cake, it's the frosting. It's not the steak, it's the salt. Have enough self-awareness to know when you're spinning out of control, and stop yourself before you end up sucking dick like a back alley prostitute in exchange for five minutes on the *Today* show.

That's the moral of the story. It's the point of this whole book, and maybe the most important thing you can learn in life: don't suck dick for five minutes on the *Today* show.

Say it slowly now, and out loud, regardless of where you are: Don't. Suck. Dick. For. Five. Minutes. On. The. *Today*. Show.

Turn to the person next to you. Look them in the eye. Don't suck dick for five minutes on the *Today* show.

Don't suck dick for five minutes on the *Today* show.

And that, my friends, is *my* lower back tattoo.

ENDNOTES

1   Berenstein, J. (2017). *I Made Up This Statistic—For This Book*. HGS: 8675309. Boston, FU: Harnard Graduate School.

2   From a high-ranking anonymous source.

3   There are thirteen distinct species of nerd, which is a member of the dork genus.

4   Interview by Chuck Todd. *Meet the Press*. NBC, January 22, 2017.

5   Reference to an obscure double murder case from 1994 involving the actor who played Jernigan in *The Towering Inferno*.

6   Interview by Bill Maher. *Real Time with Bill Maher*. HBO, September 16, 2016.

7   Interview by George Stephanopoulos. *This Week*. ABC, January 22, 2017.

8   Interview by Martha Raddatz. *This Week*. ABC, November 27, 2016.

9   She has two.

10 Interview by Anderson Cooper. *Anderson Cooper 360*. CNN, May 9, 2017.

11 Chuck Todd. *Meet the Press*. NBC, December 12, 2016.

12 Interview by Rachel Maddow. *The Rachel Maddow Show*. MSNBC, December 22, 2016.

13 Interview by Matt Lauer. The *Today* show. NBC, March 13, 2017.

14 Interview by Jake Tapper. CNN, February 7, 2017.

15 Interview by Rachel Maddow. *The Rachel Maddow Show*. MSNBC, December 22, 2016.

16 Interview by Michael Wolff. *Newseum*. April 12, 2017.

17 Interview by Seth Meyers. *Late Night with Seth Meyers*. NBC, January 10, 2017.

18 Interview by Rachel Maddow. *The Rachel Maddow Show*. MSNBC, August 24, 2016.

19 Creed? Fuck you, Jon.

20 Interview by Chuck Todd. *Meet the Press*. NBC, January 22, 2017.

21 Interview by Rachel Maddow. *The Rachel Maddow Show*. MSNBC, August 24, 2016.

22 Nick should have picked Rachel.

23 Just kidding, those are all things he actually said.

24 R.I.P.

25 Interview by Rachel Maddow. *The Rachel Maddow Show*. MSNBC, December 22, 2016.

26 Interview by Nora O'Donnell. *CBS This Morning*. CBS, September 20, 2016.

27 Interview with Judy Woodruff. *PBS NewsHour*. PBS, January 26, 2017.

28 Interview by Rachel Maddow. *The Rachel Maddow Show*. MSNBC, December 22, 2016.

29 Interview by Chris Cuomo. CNN, January 9, 2017.

30 Interview by Rachel Maddow. *The Rachel Maddow Show*. MSNBC, December 22, 2016.

31 Paraphrased from Rachel Maddow. *The Rachel Maddow Show*. MSNBC, December 22, 2016.

32 Five people died; hundreds were injured.

33 Interview by Rachel Maddow. *The Rachel Maddow Show*. MSNBC, December 22, 2016.

34 Interview by Anderson Cooper. *Anderson Cooper 360*. CNN, May 9, 2017.

35 She's alive, but her fingers died back in 1994. Doctors have yet to discover how this happened.

36 Yes, but that's not the point.

37 Interview by Charlie Rose. *CBS This Morning*. CBS, September 30, 2016.

38 Interview by Martha MacCallum. *Fox News*. Fox, June 8, 2017.

39   Interview by George Stephanopoulos. ABC, January 22, 2017.

40   Interview by Jake Tapper. CNN, February 7, 2017.

41   Interview by Matt Lauer and Savannah Guthrie. *Today*. NBC, March 13, 2017.

42   Interview by Rachel Maddow. *The Rachel Maddow Show*. MSNBC, December 22, 2016.

43   Trump auditioned in 2008 but claims it was rigged, says questions were "impossible."

44   Interview by Rachel Maddow. *The Rachel Maddow Show*. MSNBC, August 24, 2016.

45   Interview by Bill Maher. *Real Time with Bill Maher*. HBO, September 16, 2016.

46   Interview by Anderson Cooper. *Anderson Cooper 360*. CNN, May 9, 2017.

47   Interview by Anderson Cooper. *Anderson Cooper 360*. CNN, May 9, 2017.

48   Interview by Chris Matthews. *Hardball with Chris Matthews*. MSNBC, February 2, 2017.

49   Interview by Carol Costello. *CNN Newsroom with Carol Costello*. CNN, February 2, 2016.

50   Interview by Kate Bolduan and John Berman. *At This Hour*. CNN, March 8, 2016.

51   Interview by Jake Tapper. CNN, February 7, 2017.

52   Interview by Alisyn Camerota. *New Day*. CNN, September 12, 2016.

53   Interview by Nora O'Donnell. *CBS This Morning*. CBS, September 30, 2016.

54   Interview by George Stephanopoulos. ABC, January 26, 2017.

55   Interview by Alisyn Camerota. *New Day*. CNN, September 12, 2016.

56   Interview by Chuck Todd. *Meet the Press*. NBC, January 22, 2017.

57   Interview by Chris Wallace. *Fox News Sunday*. Fox, January 29, 2017.

58   Named 1992's "Fastest rapper in the world." You better ask somebody.

59

Art by Brian Patchett

60 Interview by Jake Tapper. CNN, February 7, 2017.

61 Interview by Alisyn Camerota. *New Day*. CNN, September 12, 2016.

62 Interview by Rachel Maddow. *The Rachel Maddow Show*. MSNBC, August 24, 2016.

63 Interview by Alisyn Camerota. *New Day*. CNN, September 12, 2016.

64 Interview by George Stephanopoulos. *This Week*. ABC, January 22, 2017.

65 Interview by Bill Maher. *Real Time with Bill Maher*. HBO, September 16, 2016.

66 Awesome *Escape from New York* reference.

67 I'm looking at you, MoveOn.org.

68 See footnote #4 re: obscure double murder case from 1994. The actor involved also played Allie in the movie *No Place to Hide*.

69 Interview by Rachel Maddow. *The Rachel Maddow Show*. MSNBC, August 24, 2016.

70 *CBS This Morning*. CBS, September 20, 2016.

71 *CBS This Morning*. CBS, September 20, 2016.

72 Awesome Jay-Z reference.

73 Awesome *Goonies* reference.

74 Interview by Rachel Maddow. *The Rachel Maddow Show*. MSNBC, December 22, 2016.

75 Interview by Chris Matthews. *Hardball with Chris Matthews*. MSNBC, February 2, 2017.

76   Interview by Chris Cuomo. CNN, March 13, 2017.

77   Interview by Bill Maher. *Real Time with Bill Maher.* HBO, September 16, 2016.

78   Interview by Lou Dobbs. *Fox Business.* Fox, January 26, 2017.

79   Interview by Lou Dobbs. *Fox Business.* Fox, January 26, 2017.

80   If you were born after 1998: Google "Friends," then make some popcorn and get your heart ready for the ride of its life.

81   Interview by Anderson Cooper. *Anderson Cooper 360.* CNN, October 11, 2016.

82   Interview by Rachel Maddow. *The Rachel Maddow Show.* MSNBC, December 22, 2016.

83   Interview by Chuck Todd. *Meet The Press.* NBC, December 4, 2016.

84   Interview by Chris Wallace. *Fox News Sunday.* Fox, January 29, 2017.

85   Interview by Jake Tapper. CNN, February 7, 2017.

86   Interview by Anderson Cooper. *Anderson Cooper 360.* CNN, October 11, 2016.

87   Trump, Donald J. (@realDonaldTrump). "At least 7 dead and 48 wounded in terror attack and Mayor of London says there is 'no reason to be alarmed!'" June 4, 2017, 7:31 a.m. Tweet.

88   Interview by Savannah Guthrie and Craig Melvin. *Today* show. NBC, June 5, 2017.

89   Alex Jones.

90   Interview by Chuck Todd. *Meet the Press*. NBC, January 22, 2017.

91   Interview by Chuck Todd. *Meet the Press*. NBC, January 22, 2017.

92   Interview by Seth Meyers. *Late Night with Seth Meyers*. NBC, January 10, 2017.

93   Interview by Rachel Maddow. *The Rachel Maddow Show*. MSNBC, December 22, 2016.

94   Interview by Rachel Maddow. *The Rachel Maddow Show*. MSNBC, December 22, 2016.

95   Interview by Chuck Todd. *Meet the Press*. NBC, January 22, 2017.

96   Interview by Alisyn Camerota. *New Day*. CNN, September 12, 2016

97   Interview by Rachel Maddow. *The Rachel Maddow Show*. MSNBC, December 22, 2016.